MONSTERS

AMONG

US

by

ISBN: 978-1-927828-50-2

This book is dedicated to my sister Ann, who passed away unexpectedly while I was preparing this book for publication. She died a lost soul, silent and alone, found too late, because her situation was poorly monitored. Her leaving was way too soon.

TABLE OF CONTENTS

PROLOGUE:

A new life was ahead. The wedding and consummation were still pleasant thoughts in the background, but now the future was beginning in earnest for Gemma and Sam.

The small crumbling house, with the overgrown, treed-in back yard, was on special at the real-estate office, not even up on the board, yet. The realtor only mentioned it, when they turned away at the high prices, declaring them all out of their price range.

"A bargain," the man declared. "The owner wants to unload one of his rental properties; he is getting old, and has too much to handle. He will practically give it away.

"How much can you afford?"

They should have been suspicious right there, but when they saw it, Gemma immediately called it her dream home.

Sam said; "I can landscape the yard; redo the carpets."

With a little paint, and decorative edging, Gemma could envision the end result.

How can it go wrong at twenty thousand, with housing prices so beyond our reach?

And small town life might be different, but it's do able.

****

Gemma was re-hanging the drapes in the living room; Sam had gone to see what takeout he could get at the hotel diner. Someone had told them, they made excellent pizza.

She thought she heard the back door open, but it was way too soon for Sam to be back. Believing she was mistaken, she ignored it, and lifted her foot, to step up on the small stool.

****

He entered the house like a spirit, unseen, because her back was turned.

When the couple had first moved into the tiny village, the woman had come to their attention as a prospect. The pair had already spent considerable in the businesses about town; on the flooring and carpets; paint and new windows.

He could see, they were still renovating.

He had waited impatiently for the woman to be left alone.

Now is the perfect time!

Cloaked and invisible to the naked eye, he still crept toward her cautiously. With the heavy rod in her hand, she would not have seen him, anyway.

The ungainly thing in her arms, made it impossible for her to see beneath her feet, and she miss-stepped, stumbling over the short first step up to the stool.

He pushed her; one hard shove from behind, and she went sprawling, face first into the wall.

She never realized, she lost consciousness; only seconds spanned the time between the push and the waking; but that minute of timeframe, changed her life, forever.

Rolling her quickly to her back, without mercy, he drove in the implant, up the nose cavity, shooting home the nanobot that would tag her for life.

She is ours now!

He raised her from the floor, switched her position, so she appeared to be coming off the wall, just as she was regaining her senses, and let go of her.

Then her attacker quickly fled the scene.

****

Gemma sat on the floor stunned, blood dripping on the new laundered drapes.

What just happened? I could swear someone shoved me hard from behind.

But she was just as alone, as she had been when Sam left.

I guess, I tripped, and just hit my nose against the wall. Feels like it's broken. We can't afford a medical bill...I'll just pack it until it heals.

****

Sam's money had run out.

But he'd promised Gemma to create not only the fairytale cottage, but to build a beautiful garden to go with it. And they had succeeded, searching the many nearby garden centers, from here to the city, for plants, and flower varieties; ornaments, ponds, and fountains, that would make it spectacular.

However...the cost had added up, and now, there was nothing left to finish his driveway.

He had heard tell, that at the town dump, you could have what was disposed of for free, and someone had also informed him, the municipality was resurfacing the nearby highway, and dumping the unneeded crushed rock in their landfill.

Sam was quick to ask if he might have that discarded gravel. They were overjoyed to give it to him, as it took up too much space, and would eventually need to be dealt with; all he had to do was haul it away.

The next day, Sam was just outside of town, shoveling a load of gravel into his dilapidated pickup box.

What a godsend! It would cost me a fortune, if I had to pay for this. So what if it's oily and discolored...it's free!

****

He had waited patiently to finish his job; for hours he had watched, until the man was alone. Now, he had the perfect opportunity.

Unseen, he came from behind, with the syringe in his fist, driving the injection into the meaty thigh of his victim.

To him, it will merely feel like an insect bite...

The dastardly deed was done in seconds. The stalker quickly fled, having no qualms, that he had just sentenced another man to death. After all...

Where I come from, a man's life means nothing; there are way too many men.

****

Gemma sat among her neighbors, and husband's many relatives, and friends. The full impact of what had transpired these past three months had still not registered. She simply felt numb, unable to accept that she was now alone.

Sam is dead! This isn't real!

Yet, there in the coffin was ample evidence...a cold, wax persona of the man she loved.

The cancer had appeared like a thief in the night. One minute Sam was working on his driveway, shoveling the last bit of gravel from the truck, raking it smooth, then turning away... and, vomiting the lunch, he had just eaten, on the ground.

From then on, it had been downhill all the way. He had gone downstairs to lie down in the rec-room. He thought, he had merely gotten too much sun.

But that evening, the man who would relish any dish she prepared for him, had not even wanted to look at his supper.

Before she was finished with her own meal, Sam needed to go to the emergency at the small town hospital.

Oh, why did we ever move here? Something must have been in that gravel from the dump...otherwise, how come he got so sick, so quickly?

The night they went into emergency, had been the roughest night of her life: first the ambulance ride to the city, Sam's operation, and the long hours of waiting for word. At last, in the wee hours of the morning, the physician came to the waiting room to share the prognoses.

Sam was filled with cancer. They had removed a large tumor blocking the intestines, at the cross-section between the lower and upper bowel, but when they realized there was so much more, they had simply closed him up, and left him to his death sentence. Two months, and the tumor had grown back again, to twice its original size.

Her poor lover had suffered much pain during the remaining three months of his life, bloating up like a pregnant woman about to give birth. Sometimes, to relieve the pressure, the doctors had drained up to seven liters of fluid from his belly in a week, only to have it return within days.

His last few weeks had been spent in palliative care in their small town hospital. Every day, Gemma rose at six, was there by eight, so she could help feed and wash Sam.

She spent the rest of the day watching him sleep, or reading to him, while he moved restlessly on his bed of agony.

The last afternoon, just before she went home for supper, he begged her to take him with her; he didn't want to spend his last minutes in a hospital room. He wanted to die at their storybook home...with her.

"They are giving me a pill at night," he told her. "I don't know what it's for...I don't think it's good for me."

She hadn't really paid attention to his accusation. Gemma was afraid...she didn't think she could care for him by herself.

What if he should he fall, or get worse?

She never expected it to be her last moment with him. Gemma thought they still had days.

The call had come at four o'clock in the morning.

"Your husband died about an hour ago. Would you like to come, and say goodbye?"

Gemma was so angry. She even asked, "Why didn't you call me sooner? So I could sit with him."

I didn't even get to say goodbye!

"Well...no one noticed he was gone. We could hear his loud breathing all down the hall. He was such a disturbance to the rest of the floor...we simply ignored it, blocked it out. We didn't realize, at first, he had quit..."

Dear God! He died all alone; struggling to breathe.

Gemma would never forgive herself for not being with him. But...when she thought on it further, she was almost certain, they had put him out of his misery!

However, there was no proving her suspicions.

****

The people around Gemma, seeking to display comfort, were mostly Sam's friends, and family. It had been the same at their wedding. She had only her sister, Bella; their parents had been killed in a car accident, years before.

And, Bella was seldom a comforting soul. Her version of encouragement was always ill placed at best.

"After this is over," she whispered in Gemma's ear, as the precession of mourners followed the casket out of the church, to begin the ride to the cemetery. "You'll have to get right back out there; find yourself another man to look after you. The longer you stay off the horse, the harder it'll be to get back on."

Disgusted, Gemma shook her head in rejection of what her sister implied.

No one will ever take Sam's place! There is not another like him!

Aloud, she contradicted Bella.

"He was gentle...a God-fearing man! They are a rare find these days. He would never have hurt me!"

"Yah, but he's gone, now. You have to make plans for your future. He left you with nothing."

No matter how true that was, Gemma didn't want to think on that just now.

Together, she and Sam, had created the doll house; he had slaved over the beautiful garden, the fountain, and pool. The yard now had a bench swing, a fire pit. She still had that!

He will never sit with me on that swing again, watching the fountain splash, as night descends...Oh, God. What will I do without him?

But she was too proud to let them see her cry. Crying was for private...not in public.

****

Gemma endured the funeral luncheon, feeling too distant even to relate to his brothers. Most of the people simply talked around her. They were Sam's friends and acquaintances. He had always been the out-going one; she the silent, listening wallflower, preferring to hide away in her garden.

They're just here for the free food, anyway. None of them ever tried, or cared to get to know the real me...

Sam was ever, only, my real encouragement...my support. My one true love.

But still...Gemma wouldn't let them see her weep. After all, she was too self-conscious to ever cry in public.

****

The garage sale was a success. There was little left to do. The house was sold; possession date set for next week.

She had rented an apartment in the city; the movers had already taken off, loaded with the little she felt she would need to survive.

Gemma would follow in the dilapidated pickup truck. When she was done with it, she intended to give it to Bella.

Don't need that memory haunting me.

Bella would never pay her for the vehicle, so it would just be a free gift.

Not a single neighbor had shown up to wish Gemma good luck.

Oh, well. It's as if it was all a daydream. My life with Sam, seems but a nightmare...dream yard gone...others enjoying what we built...

Gemma swallowed the lump in her throat. As she stepped into the cab of the truck, a tiny tear escaped, and travelled unnoticed down her cheek.

Chapter 1

From birth to puberty, Loni lived almost exclusively with his mother. She was of another race, and taught him many things others would not want him to know, but then, they couldn't tell what she was showing him. She was both slave, and free...mind free.

Among the things she taught him was to show mercy, forgiveness, and love; emotions the rest of his world regarded non-essential; conditions totally unfamiliar in their society.

His mother was no more than a child herself, when she gave birth to Loni. Together, they grew up, climbing the catwalks at the top of the dome, watching from above, as the workers tended the gardens that fed them.

Loni never knew his father; he had been eliminated soon after the boy was conceived, and mother, put among the unclaimed, to be taken by another partner, after she delivered.

But somehow, long after the appointed time to separate mother from son, she had managed to avoid detection.

Then the day came, when males entered the birthing quarters, to cull the older ones they had missed, tearing them away from women who had long hidden them to protect them. Most of the children went obediently, but Loni chose to fight.

In the ensuing battle, Loni accidentally knocked over a lamp filled with hot oil. The raging fire spread swiftly; took two days to put out, and when the blackened shell finally cooled, it was realized a number of females, and young infants, had perished.

This was a society in which, to ensure a clean bloodline, baby girls were never allowed to live. Instead, genetically altered women were brought in to bear the young, and the crime of killing one of these, or the males born to them, was unforgivable. Someone must pay!

It was discovered, Loni was to blame!

When they found him, for the first time in his life, the young boy learned the meaning of discipline. First, they used a round, flat, iron skillet, applying it soundly to his posterior, until he could take no more, and begged for mercy.

When his screams had quieted, and turned to mere whimpers, they took him away to the physicians. These brutal beasts held him down, one on either side, and carefully poring acid into the ear channel, intending to deafen him, burned away even the outer ear flap in the process. Loni was now scarred for life.

But, as was stated previously, Loni's mother had taught him many things. He could still understand those around him, every word they said, and...he was aware of many more facts, they would not want him to know. Extraordinary and never anticipated by this race, not admitting such a fact was possible, his people were unaware, Loni was already a telepath.

Upon his recovery, Loni was immediately put among the flawed, to work in the gardens. The youth didn't much mind that work station; he had always loved the growing things, but, from then on, his fellow workers, and the overseers, became a constant affliction in his young life.

****

"You stupid little Flaw!" exclaimed the face, at the grate, peering in at him. "What the devil you doing in there?"

Loni did not dare reveal to the overseer, that he'd spent the night in the drainage tunnel; that the separated twins, Galar and Scar, were responsible, had locked him in.

The pair always worked together to corner him. Even though missing a leg, Galar was quick on his crutch, using his arms to trap, or send his victim close to that one powerful arm Scar had left. Twice Loni's weight, and both, taller than he, the bullies found great pleasure in tormenting the supposed deaf-mute.

With an exaggerated movement, the overseer unlocked from the outside, the barred gate covering the drain tube. Swinging it outward, he motioned for Loni to step out.

"You stupid male, don't you realize you could drowned in there?"

Loni peered around the corner of his prison, not quite ready to accept that his oppressors had finally gone away, half expecting, at least Galar, to be nearby waiting.

"Get you back to the sleep quarters!" impatiently ordered his liberator, with a growl. "And... as your punishment, you'll miss the morning feed. You'll also lose your liberty for this day. Stay within the bounds of your work area. No recreation period! Do you understand?"

As he stepped out, and started to leave, Loni nodded agreement, but immediately knew the other didn't see. He was used to being punished, whether guilty or not, and also, being treated as if he were too slow to answer.

"What's the point talking to it," a second voice chided. "You forget, that's the deaf-mute? Of course, he won't understand."

That was when, Loni realized, another man stood behind the first. They always did walk the beat in pairs.

The first supervisor shrugged his shoulders. "I never have trouble directing him..."

But the second disagreed again. "We'll need to watch this idiot closer; he gets into too much trouble. Don't know what good he is; they should just put him down."

"He's my best worker, has an instinct for what needs doing, a connection to the plants...like he's one with the garden produce...besides, he doesn't complain."

The other laughed, seeing a joke in every word spoken. Both men took Loni by an arm, lifted him off his feet, and with him in tow, made for the work stations.

****

Some ten years later:

Loni still grieved the loss of his sister, and mother. He knew she had recently died birthing a girl child; the constant awareness of her, and the many thought-words of encouragement had ceased in his head.

At the moment, he stood at the side of the physician, a guard on either side of him; awaiting the results of his annual physical. They had just taken the last blood sample.

He wasn't sure why they were doing all the scans this time...

Perhaps, it's because they consider me an adult now?

Loni had developed into a heavily muscled giant of over six feet, and thought himself rather handsome...except for the scars where his ears should have been, which he covered self-consciously with his curly white-blond hair.

He knew, they would never allow him to have a partner...they considered him to be flawed.

"I sure hope they don't use the blood samples from one of these," objected the one guard to the other, as they led

Loni away. "The alter-cloning process is fragile, and selective enough, without using the inferior."

"And what would you know of the procedure, anyway?" asked the other.

"I listen to the physicians talk...when I'm here."

The other laughed. "So do I. They seldom use the flawed ones' samples, only if..."

"If what?"

"If the male is of an exceptional DNA..."

"Such as?"

"Perhaps, of a blood group compatible to all..."

"Well, that makes little sense, when he's already flawed. Will they put him with a partner, if one develops? Why should they have a mate, when most of us go without? Surely, they will castrate him? The female would also be flawed. Instead, they should both be put down."

The other seemed to agree. " Most definitely! But, consider this: where would we get future workers, if these were not allowed to reproduce?"

"You mean, they deliberately create flawed females for the workers?"

The other shrugged.

Their words enraged Loni; in his mind, he was fuming.

I was not born flawed! You are the ones who made me this way!

My mother was a perfect one! I'd like to see you top her! And, she said, my father was of the gentle kind...a rarity. I come from good blood!

You are the dense ones...judging whether I live or die!

Chapter 2

Gemma didn't believe it! It was just too surreal! Lightning simply didn't strike twice in the same place. But it had...

Sam's death had never quite been forgotten, but she had finally put it behind her, and was ready to date again. Gemma had never remarried; she saw nothing remotely out there to measure up to her one true love, and so, she was more or less a loner, concentrating on career and a quiet life. She had few friends, preferring to keep to herself.

No! I cannot have caught it from Sam. It's been ten years! This isn't the same; it's just a glitch to slow me down, now that I have finally decided to venture out again.

When it started, Gemma believed it was just an allergy. Her nose seemed always to be dripping, or plugged, and having to mouth-breathe was not pleasant. But it was nothing serious.

Her eyes became swollen, and sight diminished, until it was extremely difficult to see, unless the print was enlarged, especially when working at the computer. But...it was only an infection.

Then came the pounding sinus headache just across the bridge of her nose. That was near impossible to bear.

Yet, she still denied it; thought it just an allergy cold...or maybe, the flu.

It is flu season, and I haven't gotten a shot yet.

And then, the nausea hit. Her mouth was filled with cotton; her throat sore. She couldn't swallow; couldn't eat. The weight dropped from her like water. Thirty-five pounds!

At last, feeling too ill to take a bus by herself, Gemma called her sister, Bella, to drive her to the hospital emergency.

And that was when, she was struck the final blow.

****

They went to the nearest facility. But, the ER doctor there stereotyped her, along with all the usual patrons, seeking care in the area of this particular hospital.

This was skid row; a hangout for derelicts wanting a place to shelter. The coffee shop, and waiting rooms were always overflowing with people from the street, watching TV, while warming up.

The attitude was one of contempt, as if the attendant had seen one too many patients faking it, and Gemma was the last straw. The doctor assumed, she was just another native drug-addict, after pain medication to take the edge off withdrawal. It was common knowledge, some of those that came by, even used their intravenous ports for a quick way to get high; that site introduced it directly into the vein.

But Gemma was neither Métis, nor pure blood aboriginal. Though born here, and third generation, she was blond, and obviously Caucasian. Still, it didn't matter.

With Bella sitting in a chair by her side, Gemma lay on a cot, for hours, waiting to be seen.

The blood work finally ordered; samples taken; she was scrutinized by three nurses, each examining her eyes, judging their focus, before the physician even put in an appearance. Then, giving the test results a mere cursory glance, he simply declared, there was nothing wrong with her.

If it hadn't been for the head nurse with him, he would have simply walked away, dismissing her.

"Look at her eyes," argued the woman. "They don't even track. That's not normal. There is something else wrong! She needs a CT scan."

"Fine!" he declared, just to get her off his back. "Do the scan, then."

****

The voice on the other end of the telephone held barely disguised excitement.

"I have discovered a tagged," he proclaimed to the listener. "But, they must have lost track of her, for she has been severely neglected. The site is infected...what should I do?"

"The process, as with any other, is the same. Give her the diagnoses, and refer her to the centre."

"Okay. Is there any reward for having found her?"

"Such as what?"

"Well...like...being pushed further up the list..." stuttered the other.

"Do your duty well, and it may be considered. But, this is no different than anyone else. Your call has been noted; that will be all."

The line on the other end went dead; there was no chance to argue the point.

****

Gemma and Bella were moved to a private room, the curtains drawn, so no one could see in. Both women wondered why.

Gemma immediately had a premonition of foreboding.

After a time, the ER Attending slunk in with his charts, as if suddenly ashamed of his previous behavior. He closed the door; slowly took a seat; shuffled his papers, and at last, looked up. But, he seemed to be appealing to Bella; not looking directly at Gemma, as though he were asking forgiveness for an act about to be perpetrated.

"I'm afraid I have some bad news," he apologized. "We found a tumor growing behind the eye..."

Gemma felt annoyed.

The real bad news, is it took you so long to listen!

To her, tumor meant a growth. It could be removed; treated, whatever it took.

Nothing serious. I can go through this, as long as it's gone when we are done.

But, Bella was a homecare worker; she knew a little more about the medical implications. It was she, alone, who realized the full impact of his words.

"You have some decisions to make, so I'll leave you alone for a moment to discuss your options," the doctor decided. "I'll come back later with a referral...if that should be the route you wish to take."

His clipboard in his hands, he hurriedly left the room.

Gemma didn't know what to think. When she turned to look at Bella, her sister was in tears.

"Oh, Gemma...I'm so sorry...but...I just can't do this!"

Whatever is she talking about?

It wasn't until after further tests, and treatment had begun, that Gemma realized the death sentence inflicted upon her.

And, that was the last time she ever saw her sister.

Chapter 3

"This is a tagged one?"

Two physicians were viewing the CT scan of a woman in her thirties.

"We've told her it's a tumor..."

"It has developed considerable growth around the nano-tag. It must have been placed at least ten years ago. How did we lose track of her?"

"Not important. We have her back, now."

"So...what is the procedure?"

"We give it to the guys in oncology. There are enough of us posing as specialists to direct her treatment, and change. She'll have the same basic therapy as any other cancer patient; should go unnoticed among them."

"How does it work?"

"We simply kill all her normal cells, then introduce the donor DNA."

"She's a bit older than we usually use..."

"No matter...sure, on one this age, it is still experimental, but...if it takes..."

"Aw...yes. Here's hoping."

****

"Ump...umm...umm," sounded constantly, on a three tonal descending scale, throughout the vast room. Not just one pump, but four, and never a one in sync. It was like a death knell all night long, and not just while you tried to sleep, but all day, as well.

"Ump...umm...umm," from the machines that pumped the poisons into their systems. One visitor had said it sounded like the sound of a chickadee, but then she was a farmer's wife, and could be excused. Truth was, if only it was the sound of a song bird, and not an instrument meant to save, or take, their lives. All four in the ward were hooked up to one, continually.

At night, exhausted, the patients tried to sleep. Combined with the constant clicking of binders closing, at the nearby nurses station, was the constant snoring of a neighbor in the next bed, who would start awake, then return to opened-mouth breathing, and soon, once again to the rhythm. But the one most sonorous was the mother of the sixteen year old native boy, in the bed next to Gemma. The poor woman was trying to rest in a wide sleep-chair made of leather, and every time she moved, it groaned as if a living thing. Most uncomfortable, too.

The boy had testicular cancer. It had been caught early, and he was the only one in the room with a definite chance of survival. He usually had a day pass; would walk the malls with his relatives all day, then come back for his deadly venom, four hours of treatment, at night.

It was three o'clock in the morning, and though it was already April, outside the windows, snow fell like a curtain, obliterating in a white-out any scenery: parking lot, rooftops, the park and river beyond.

At least I have the window bed.

Gemma couldn't sleep. From another room, she could hear an old man cursing the staff. He wanted to get up and use the washroom, but the Chemo had addled his brain so badly, he didn't know where he was, and he thought, they were his children, being mean. It had been going on all night.

What a way to spend my birthday! I should be out celebrating with Bella. Thirty is a milestone...I wonder if she will visit me today?

Morning came, and with it breakfast. Gemma dreaded anything concerning food. Her mouth and throat were so sore, it was a constant struggle to eat. Every morsel gagged her. It seemed, she had contracted Thrush, a mouth infection some patients developed while receiving Chemo.

In the bed across from her was Adrian; sixty-three, over six foot five, emaciated, bald; a diabetic with stage four Cancer. They were giving him his poison in a continuous stream for seventy-two hours.

Because of this, he ate continuously, to keep his blood sugar up. His favorite phrase was: 'what you got on your tray?' He liked to trade, but Gemma simply gave him what she couldn't stomach.

The hardest part was when his girl friend came to visit. She showed up leaden down with all manner of fresh fruits, and goodies, generously offering, the lady in the bed across, a sampling. Oh, how Gemma longed to eat; she even dreamed of food when she did doze off, but she always refused their savory treats, because she knew, she couldn't chew or swallow.

Trouble was, this couple were like the devil having an argument with God. Adrian was constantly complaining, criticizing the lot he'd been given, those who were trying to help him, and everyone in general. No one did anything right.

His poor friend did her best to cheer him, but he was so bitter; could see nothing good in his future, and in his words, 'What good is all this? Just to buy a few years. What quality of life will I have, in and out of hospital all the time?'

What really got to Gemma was his attitude toward religion. He mocked any support system, volunteer or funded. He said, he refused to celebrate Christmas or Easter; it was just a grab for money. "If there was a creator, the least he could do is come down here, and show us that he cared."

Gemma looked around her. Everywhere, nurses scurried, tending to patients' every whim. Orderlies washed the floors, emptied wastebaskets. The CCAs emptied the pee pots, changed their beds every day, even gave each patient a bath and clean gown every morning.

If God isn't down here, in the persons of these people, ministering to us, showing His love, how are they able to continue doing it day after day?

But Adrian felt he was a logical man; he would rather believe we evolved from monkeys, than admit to something Omnipotent and benevolent. After all, he had been a teacher all his life, and he'd never yet seen evidence of a creator.

All his life, maybe, the cancer has affected his eyes?

In the bed beside this atheistic man, was the fourth patient residing in the room. Benny was terminal; a tumor invading his brain. His memory came and went, and he had to be retold simple facts that had previously been discussed.

In a room such as this, every word said by patients, or visitors alike, was public knowledge; impossible to miss. Privacy was nil. Gemma listened, as his daughter, and her female partner, loudly discussed his coming to live with them for the few days of life he had left. The delay, they told him, over and over, was his son, who had power of attorney, and refused to release the funds. He didn't trust his sister. Benny had been waiting in hospital for thirty days.

Between what she heard from Benny and his family, and Adrian and his girl friend, Gemma found it extremely difficult to remain positive. It had shocked her at first, just to realize, the ward was co-ed, let alone to be thrown into the lives of other people like this. Gemma had always been a private person, only interacting when she chose. To be forced to face not only this new actuality, but the truth of her own diagnoses at the same time, simply rocked her world; sent her spinning into depression. All she wanted was to get out of there.

No amount of exercise, or good eating could change the death sentence she had been handed. Suddenly, she had no control over anything, especially, her own physical health. It terrified the young woman, as she realized, even if this Cancer were eradicated, it could return again at any time.

And the deep emersion bath into this multinational oncology floor, with its doctors, nurses, and other attendants, coming from every race and creed conceivable, severed Gemma's touch with her own comfortable reality.

****

Five days had past. Even though in the communal ward, Gemma was lonely. She felt envious, as she watched the constant stream of visitors to her patient companions. They brought gifts, reading material, foods of all kinds: take out; milk shakes; fruit; chocolates. They stayed and sat with their friend, or family member, even while that person dozed away the day. A constant hum of visitation passed back and forth between the beds. Everyone knew the history of the other, sympathized and encouraged...except, where she was concerned.

Gemma never received a card, text or phone call, and nor any visitors; no one worried over her welfare.

Finally, desperate for some attention, Gemma sent her sister, Bella, a text:

'I feel so alone; abandoned. Are you out there? Do you even care?'

The cell phone remained silent. There was no answering text; no word of encouragement, support...or even a reassuring, 'I love u.'

****

That first stay in the hospital lasted eight days. Every day, Gemma begged her doctor to release her. All she wanted to do was be back in her little apartment nest, left alone, so she could become grounded again in her own reality.

But, what is reality now? This feels like I'm dying.

Finally, against his better judgment, the physician set her free. They needed the bed for another patient. There never were enough beds to service the need in oncology.

The ride home in the taxi was torturous. Though they had managed to deal with her Thrush, and she could eat, somewhat, Gemma was still terribly nauseous. With the swaying of the vehicle, the way the driver speedily negotiated the treacherous turns, all occurrences appeared exaggerated to her. So ill did she feel, she was certain that at any minute, before this ride was over, she would baptize the taxi driver's inner sanctum.

At last, she stood before her home building, and had managed not to vomit all over the cab interior.

Once inside her small apartment, it seemed unfamiliar; she had been away that long. Gemma could hardly stay standing long enough to put away the coat she wore.

Through the following days, most of her time was spent lying on the couch. Each deed she did was interspersed by a periods of rest on the sofa; then up again to complete what she started. When she managed to make and eat a meal, it came up again, until at last, the anti-nausea drugs, they had sent home with her, began to kick in.

And added to all this, came a new problem. Gemma hardly had the energy to take her bath. Again she needed to lie down before she could even towel off. But the ultimate shock came while bathing; there was more hair than liquid in the tub. All her beautiful golden waves were coming out by the handful.

Now, Gemma understood why the patients around her had all been bald. Chemo made the hair fall out.

It was more a blow to her pride than anything else. A mirror, now, was her worst enemy!

I look so ugly! Who would ever look at me now? Leave alone, want to spend their life with me.

She hadn't really listened, and definitely didn't believe it now, when they had told her, it would grow back thicker, white, and curly.

The prospect of dating was a thing of the past...

Regrets were pointless; she had wasted ten years grieving, and now it was too late.

After a week at home, Gemma began to feel much better, but not strong enough for the second round of Chemo which was coming up soon.

Two weeks later, her entire mindset had reversed. She missed her bed companions, and the constant visitation in the common room. From wanting to be by herself, she now felt comforted by the thought, there would be nursing staff to wait on her.

At least, when I'm there, I won't die all alone. There is always someone, to answer the press of a button, to come to my aid.

Just when she was back on her feet...dreading the next round of poison, Gemma again reported to the oncology ward.

That beastie in my nose has got to go! There is no avoiding this!

Trouble was the toxin couldn't differentiate between the human, and wayward cells. It killed all, indiscriminately.

Chapter 4

"This one's no good for anything!" the irate supervisor declared disgustedly, pushing the worker forward ahead of him. "I've given him the moniker, 'no-name'; it certainly suits him. You can't even communicate with him; he just stands there. Dah! Stupid, or what?"

"Here, let's try him with Flaw. If anyone can do something with a moron, he can."

The first man grinned. "Figures...a deaf-mute and an idiot. They'll fit just right." With that, he grabbed the unfortunate youth by the ear, and dragged him, moaning and struggling, over to where Loni was weeding.

Loni raised his eyes; sat back on his haunches. Their victim was about five years his junior, a short fellow, not much over five foot tall, with a shock of black hair, and an infantile face. He appeared not more than a child, but when Loni searched his mind, he realized his correct age.

He also, quickly knew, the real reason the fellow couldn't communicate: the words of others were simply garbled to his ears. There was a gap between the message receptors in his brain, and he didn't get the meaning.

The Super made sure Loni was looking at him before he spoke. They assumed, he could read lips.

"Make this one work, Flaw!" he shouted, as if that would make the order more comprehensible. "Do you understand?"

Loni nodded.

The two overseers stood there for a moment to make certain the two could interact.

Loni moved the new boy to a position across from him, showed him what were weeds, and what were not. Then by exaggerated example, pulled a weed, and tossed it in the pail. it was as simple as that.

"Well, guess you were right," laughed the first man, as the two moved away. "I couldn't get him to do anything; never thought to show him."

When their guardians were out of sight, Loni probed the mind of his fellow worker, so he could understand him better. The younger man had been greatly abused from the moment he could stand. When they'd realized he was incommunicative; he was called names, pushed, kicked, dunked, all to try to get him to obey.

He had given himself the name 'Da'. He had heard it so often, regarding himself, he had taken it to mean, that was the name they called him. That made Loni sad, and he resolved to treat this new coworker with dignity.

I will protect you, Da.

He didn't realize he had projected the thought, until Da smiled at him.

He can understand me!

****

For the first time in his life, Loni felt he had a friend. Da was like a younger brother.

The illusion was further enhanced by the fact they were placed together in the sleep accommodations. Between that, and working together side-by-side daily, the two men became fast friends, and inseparable, though their communication only went one way. Loni was the telepath; though he tried, he couldn't teach Da his talent.

Everyone now called them Flaw and No-name, but Loni much preferred, they be called Da and Flaw, if there was to be any name calling. However, he couldn't correct the name aloud, and he had to leave their version stand.

Loni's constant scourge, from childhood, soon discovered them, and could not resist temptation.

At a very young age, Galar and Scar had been placed in a private sleep room by themselves. Perhaps, this was due to the fact, they had been born as one unit, and after the physicians separated them, the boys appeared lost without each other, and incapable of functioning alone.

Now that Loni had someone as well, Galar appeared to take offense to the fact. It seemed, he thought, such a thing was the twins' exclusive right. From the moment Da appeared, Galar made it his life purpose, to not only make life miserable for the newcomer, but to drive Flaw and Da apart.

Loni did not lose his temper easily; he chose not to react, having had years of previous experience with this bully. But Da was easy to pick on. Whenever these separated twins had a moment of idleness, they slipped away to Loni's work site.

One time, it was time to harvest the apples. As did everyone else, Da carried his pouch suspended about his neck and over his chest, to keep his hands free. He had a full bag, when Galar came from behind him, and upended it, with a quick push from the bottom.

Da usually imitated Loni; it was his habit not to react. Loni had also taught him, again through example, to express pleasure, discouragement, and even disapproval, by a series of tonal grunts. Then, he would simply go on with what he was doing.

But, after several times of losing his load, and having to pick each individual fruit again from the ground, Da's patience was wearing thin. The last time, his grunt was definitely not one of discouragement, alone. This one was of anger!

And Loni didn't blame him.

Da began to holler, something no one had heard him do before. His scream of frustration carried over the work site, attracting the guards. And Galar stood nearby, beside himself with glee, at his accomplishment. He felt assured, surely now, these two would be parted.

But the overseers were not stupid! Da seldom made trouble. And Galar was obviously away from his appointed picking area.

For once, Galar was the one punished. He was forbidden to come anywhere near where the pair was working, and this angered Galar immensely, but...he had waited for revenge before. He could bide his time again.

At this point in time, Da and Loni were still bunked in the communal sleep area. It was here Galar chose to enact his next retribution.

When either of the pair slipped between the sheets, they would be short-sheeted, or sopping wet. Galar must have entered while the cleaning crew was changing bedding. Doing his thing, was no doubt the amusement of the day.

Sometimes, Da found a toad or a lizard in his pillow slip, but what finally got to Loni, was one night, when the younger man found he had no bed at all. Da whined in misery, slunk down where the mat should have been, and curled up against the wall, with great tears forming in his large, expressive eyes.

Loni knew the boy was unusually tired that day from the heavy day's labors. This was the last straw, and it made his blood boil to see Da so tormented.

Marching determinedly to the door, he meant to deal with Galar, once and for all. He never made it.

Their two original caretakers had watched the whole thing.

The foursome had been under observation for some time, their supervisors laughing at the constant battering the younger pair took, waiting to see, just what it would take, for the one they called 'Flaw', to react.

They never bargained, he would actually have a breaking point.

Before Loni could reach the hall, each overseer grabbed him by an arm, and brought him up short. They were large bulky men, and held the muscular 'Flaw' suspended above the floor, but Loni still fought them valiantly.

They shook him; turned him to face them, and the one shouted in his face.

"Stop it, Flaw! We'll deal with this."

Without any further ado, they propelled him forward to his mat, and unceremoniously, dumped him there. Then, the sleep quarters went into lockdown; no one in or out for the night.

"These are my best workers!" declared the Super, as the two went out the door. "I can't have them wasting energy fighting!"

When the door was closed, and the lights dimmed, Loni motioned to Da to join him. The younger one climbed in beside him, and together they slumbered so, for the night, Loni curled against Da's back, spoon-like.

The next night, the pair called 'No name' and 'Flaw' were given a private room. Ever after, their door was always barred, day and night, from intruders.

Chapter 5

"I am so sick of this!" complained the short chubby Asian CCA to her companion. "We are forever emptying her pee hat. Where does she get it all? She must drink gallons during the day to void so much at night."

"I've already put in a complaint to her physician. He said to restrict her fluid intake. No water after seven at night, and only one pitcher of ice-water during the day. Her electrolytes drop too low."

"That will teach her," laughed the other.

"She still struggles with Thrush," a third broke in, in the patient's defense. "The reason she drinks so much is because it eases her dry mouth and nausea."

"Then give her the anti-nausea medication."

"She refuses to take meds she feels she doesn't need," countered the other. "Says, they add to her dry mouth. She wasn't one to take drugs prior to this; has an allergy to some drugs, especially those for pain."

"Oh, posh! That's all something in her head," disagreed the first. "Her dry mouth is because she breathes through her mouth at night; the tumor blocks her nose."

"None of that matters. We follow doctor's orders. No water..."

****

For two nights and a day, Gemma had been wondering why the water girls would give her a jug of ice-water, and immediately the nurse or CCA would snatch it away. When she asked, she was told, her void and intake were being monitored; fluid ingestion recorded; after every meal, they even counted every glass of juice and milk.

But night time was the worst.

I can't take this anymore! If they won't give me water, I'll just steal it from the tap in the bathroom.

Gemma hid the Styrofoam cup in the folds of her hospital gown, pushing the pole of the IV along the floor toward the bathroom. It was almost four in the morning, and the nurse was nowhere in sight. She knew it was soon time for the Chemo bag to be replaced; they always woke her to do it.

But she needed to drain...and desperately craved water. She would do anything to get it!

Yet, when she had accomplished the deed, it seemed a pointless endeavor. The liquid hadn't done much to alleviate the problem. Gemma was still dying of thirst.

Finally, at six AM someone took pity on her, giving her a jug of water. By shift change at eight, she had drank most of it, afraid they would snatch it away, when the new girls came on.

****

It was finally morning. The nurses from both shifts were in review.

Gagging, Gemma swiftly sat up in the hospital bed. Something was slowly slipping from her nose, down her throat. She leaned far forward, but it failed to stop what was happening.

She coughed hard, grabbed at a tissue from the box on the table at her side. Gasping to catch a breath, she gagged violently again.

Whatever was in there, now slid to the top of her windpipe, cutting off the air completely.

For this round, Gemma was in the bed nearest the door. A nurse appeared from the nursing station directly across; stood in the doorway, watching, a worried look on her face. Desperately struggling to breathe, Gemma was completely unaware of this concerned observer.

Coughing, retching, she finally gagged the obstruction up, and spit it into the soft paper in her hand.

Gemma opened her fist, staring at the thing lying there: a large gob of greenish-gray; square...like a metal chip, and hard.

What the heck! Is this part of my tumor?

"Are you alright?" asked the nurse, approaching the bedside.

Gemma held out what she had regurgitated; the woman turned away, repulsed. She didn't seem much inclined to examine the thing further.

"I nearly choked..."

"I know. We were watching from the nursing station. We had no idea how to help you. I'm glad, you're okay."

Only then, did Gemma become aware of the crowd gathered in the doorway. Quickly the rest of the staff turned back to the work they had been doing.

Oh, man! I've had an audience. How embarrassing!

****

"She's lost her tag," revealed the orderly to the head physician. "We all watched from the nurses' station as she almost choked, gagging it up. It had grown too large to pass down the throat. We wouldn't have a problem, if it had been smaller; would just have passed into the stomach and adhered to the wall. Now, instead, she has no tag."

With little show of sympathy, the doctor retorted: "Well, see she is tagged again. We have done too much with her, to be stymied, now. We can't be losing her!"

"Where should we tag her, and...how?"

"Try her IV site."

****

Gemma was so uncomfortable she felt like crying. For days, she had tried to get the nurse to look at her IV site; it ached like heck! But, nobody listened...until it was too late.

Now she was on antibiotics, with an infected wrist. Each time, they had to squeeze the wound to extract the puss, before applying the ointment, and wrapping the area.

It will leave a scar now, for the rest of my life!

****

"Her body rejects any tag we try to introduce," complained the orderly. "The IV site is badly infected, and her veins are rolling. She's almost impossible to plant another IV; covered with bruises from where we've tried...we are going to lose this one, if we don't take other measures."

"Okay," decided the physician. "We'll give her the blood transfusion. I'll see you get the compatible supply..."

As the orderly turned to go, the other stopped him with a word.

"See that she's tagged properly, after. Try it orally..."

"She's leery; questions everything we do..."

"Tell her, she's low in potassium..."

The other nodded, and went to carry out his orders.

****

Loni and Da were weeding out the portulaca in the flower beds, throwing the prolific plants in a pail to die, before they were burned in the refuse. The two controllers surprised them, coming out of nowhere, grabbing Loni by either arm, as was their custom, and starting off with him in tow. Loni had been intent on his thoughts, deep in mental concentration, listening in to the minds of the healthcare personal in the adjacent lab-room; he hadn't even sensed the presence of his overseers.

"Come on, Flaw!" declared the rougher handler on his right. "It's your turn to give. They have need for more blood."

Oh, not again! I just gave two days ago. Why always me?

"It's no use telling him," his companion remonstrated. "He's not looking at you, so he can't understand. Remember, he's this freak of nature that's deaf to all we say."

These two must be new. It's been a while since they belittled me this way.

"Why they even want his blood, then?" demanded the other. "I thought the flaws weren't allowed companions?"

"They usually aren't, but every once in a while we get a reject, a difficult case they've put a lot into, and don't want it to go to waste. Anyway, Flaw is of cross-mix blood. He can give blood to any new one developing."

"You'd think that would result in a flawed one?"

The other shrugged. "What do I know about it? Let the docs do their thing. They can deal with the consequences; it's their experiment, and...they're learning new things each day."

Chapter 6

"Arch your back! Like a cat!" ordered the large, solid man behind Gemma.

She tried to comply, but she wasn't certain what he meant. She pushed out her belly.

"No! Not in!" he commanded gruffly. "Out! I can't get the needle between the vertebrae. Do you want me to cripple you?"

His anger was apparent, though Gemma knew doctor Harmon wasn't usually this curt. He was the more gentle of the physicians caring for her. But, she was small, compared to him, half his girth, and she'd always been afraid of larger men.

Yet, he was the only one in whose eyes she'd ever seen compassion; the others all looked at her like she was something growing in a Petri dish, and they were watching through the microscope.

Gemma moved her hips backward, toward the physician.

"That's better!"

To break the silence that followed, as he swabbed, then injected the freezing, Gemma tried to explain.

"I didn't understand before, but now...I do."

"Hold still..."

She was seated on a stool, leaning forward, her arms on a pillow atop the bed, with Doctor Harmon behind her, so she wouldn't see the huge needle coming. But Gemma felt when it punctured the skin; the numbness wasn't quite complete.

He drove it deeper, and she held her breath.

To keep from thinking about what was happening at her back, her mind went to the many unanswered questions.

Why am I the only one who gets my treatment in the spine? I still get all the chemicals the others get intravenously, but I get this, too. I've never seen them do a spinal on anyone else.

****

Where he came from, they were taught not to be emotional. Emotion was deadly! It caused you to break cover.

But unlike the others stationed here, the one who called himself, Doctor Harmon, had learned the pretext of showing compassion; sometimes, it wasn't all put on either. He really didn't like to see this one hurt.

When he'd seen her IV site festering, he knew drastic measures were needed, but he couldn't do it himself. Even when the nurse was squeezing out the puss, he had turned away, so as not to watch. He knew the patient had seen the tears forming in his eyes, before he could hide them.

And his weakness angered him.

Surely, there is an easier way to form what we want; why must we torment them so?

This one was so full of questions. Right now, she had another one, he found hard to counter.

"How come, I have to have this procedure in my back? Are there others who get it this way?"

How can I tell her? She is receiving foreign altered cells from an alien donor?

He thought quickly, fabricating according to the diagnoses she'd been given.

"Because the tumor is in the sinus area, we need to get to it as quickly as possible. The straightest course is directly into the spinal fluid, up to the brain, and into the nasal area."

She was quiet, then; satisfied.

Why must they be so trusting? This one believes nothing without being given the reason. Yet, she has faith in me. Why? I am no different than the others. Is it my manner...the sympathy? Perhaps, this trait is not wise to portray?

If she only knew what I am actually doing to her...she would run so far from me; never let me touch her again.

****

"All done," the physician declared, pulling shut her gown, giving her shoulder a pat, and pushing away from behind Gemma.

He moved away so quickly, as if he didn't wish to interact further, and had disappeared around the corner, before she could turn around.

At least it didn't hurt. But, now for the more difficult part.

She was required to lie flat on her back on the bed, her head lower than her feet, not moving, for an hour. The hardest part would be holding her water that long.

Gemma sighed resignedly, and got up onto the bed. The nurse lowered the head-end of her cot.

At least, I went potty in their stupid hat before my treatment!

It seemed to her, she was always filling that annoying thing, that up-side-down pot, that fit into the stool. The nurses called it a hat, and that's just what it looked like...all, so they could measure her output. It was so utterly public!

Embarrassing!

Chapter 7

At last, Gemma was back at home!

Three weeks between each treatment.

But, what they had failed to prepare her for, was that there would be extended hospital stays. During the three separate encounters, when she added them together, she had spent nearly five weeks on the hospital oncology floor.

First, it had been the Thrust; then, the infected IV site, and this last time, something had gone very wrong with her heart. It now had a new crazy beat.

The nurses, at first, had considered it amusing, an anomaly, something they marveled at, that was actually audible to their ears. It was like she had a second sleeper heart behind her own organ; every couple of beats came an echo. Gemma could feel it when it happened. It caught her breath...actually hurt.

A specialist was called in. He came with a parade of interns, each listening to the bizarre beat, amazed at the phenomenon, but none seemed the least bit alarmed.

After a sonogram; more blood tests, and even a full body PET scan, the head professional prescribed a medication that seemed to calm the unusual sound, hushing that extra echo, so it was no longer in evidence.

When the physician came back alone to her bedside, he told Gemma, it was nothing to worry about; everything was proceeding as planned. She took him at his word, leaving the hospital, without giving it another thought.

She had her medication; all would be fine.

If they don't feel it is dangerous, then why should I worry?

Trouble was, when she looked at the prescription bottle she realized, it had no refill, and she'd been given only a month's supply.

Now, what's up with that?

****

They had told her; next step was radiation, and true to their word, these treatments began two weeks later. First, she was fitted with a confining mask that formed to her features. She was to lay on the hard metal table, her eyes shut, the apparatus strapped over her entire face; it was clamped to the table, as well, so she couldn't get free if she'd wanted to.

Everyone left the room, and for fifteen minutes, Gemma listened to the noises of a room she couldn't see. The machines clunked into position, whirled around her, constantly changing location, again and again. Each time she was aware of the red beam moving over her face. If it went elsewhere, she couldn't tell.

It never hurt. Though, when she returned home after the sessions, her nose had a continual bloody drip...nothing alarming, only annoying, for it drained down her throat at night, giving her a constant cough.

This new department wasn't at all like oncology, where the attention of the nurses and CCA's were ever there to see to your needs. Here, they seemed to feel, you were at their beck and call. An appointment could change at a moment's notice, and you were expected to be available. If it had not been for the volunteer drivers who chauffeured her, Gemma would have missed many an appointment.

Actually it was one of those drivers who over booked, nearly causing Gemma to be late. In the end, they sent a taxi instead.

The first taxi driver was indeed a character. He told her, he was fasting for a month long religious festival. He couldn't eat or drink from sunup until darkness; not even a sip of water, but after nine-thirty at night, his people could eat anything they wanted; could even pig-out until morning, if they choose. The thought brought Gemma up short.

That isn't fasting! Not when you can eat all you want in the evening. You are just changing the time of your meal.

"Why?" she asked.

"To remind us, there are others who go without food."

Gemma was appalled.

And they do this all month? He can't even drink...all day long, and HE is driving me? My life is in HIS hands!

Am I safe?

The second time she was forced to take a cab, that driver extolled the benefits of his beliefs; told her, because she was suffering so much, she was assured of making it into paradise.

Because each new driver seemed to be an immigrant from another country, Gemma got the uncanny feeling she was being watched, scrutinized and graded.

Where are all our home grown people; those who were born here? Are all the jobs only given to the foreigners?

Thankfully, the help program didn't fail her too often.

****

Doctor Gee removed the chart from the pocket in the door, opened it, and stopped short in surprise. He was so used to this by now; most patients being utterly pointless, but here was a tagged one, a prospect he could consider.

I am so tired of serving here. How many years have I been buried in their society? I long to find my partner, and go back home.

If this one is at all suitable, I will cut my loses. Fifty years is too long to be waiting!

Apparently, he had seen this one several times.

Why did I not notice her status before? Perhaps, because there is always another female worker in the room distracting me?

He opened the door; walked forward, hand outstretched to take hers.

She appeared ashamed of her bald head, usually keeping it covered with some sort of kerchief, but today she had removed the covering, anticipating that he would want to see into her eyes.

Why she's beautiful! This one is it! I will remove her from the system, so no one else can have her!

****

Her treatments had continued every day for a full five weeks.

Gemma most detested when she must be examined by the attending physician. Once a week, the man reviewed her progress, sticking a probe up her nose as if he were enjoying her discomfort. He stood over her, with the band holding the lamp around his forehead, oblivious to the fact it was blinding her with its brightness.

He was an elderly gentleman, who appeared totally out of it, seemed away in some other dimension. Sometimes, he peered around the room as though it was unfamiliar, as if he wasn't certain of where he was. Though he had met her a couple of times, interviewed her at the beginning, he never seemed to remember that he had.

Nor did he ever listen to her complaints. It didn't matter what she told him, he simply ignored it. Gemma had learned, it was useless to answer the question: 'How are you today?' He didn't want an answer.

It was always: "Everything is progressing beautifully."

Are you kidding me? My nose is constantly bleeding; my ear is infected. Can't you see? You say, this is normal?

But today was the worst. He stood grinning like a Cheshire cat, as if he could eat her, should she let him.

"This is the last visit before you are finished," he stated. "Your treatments will be over in two days."

Gemma knew it was pointless to ask him, what was to happen next.

****

That Friday, Gemma had the last of her radiation therapy. She was so glad when it was over.

It was customary to ring the bell on the wall in the hall, to tell everyone you had survived, and finished your treatments. Gemma gave it a joyful tug as she went on by, but...

Though it resounded through the department, it was too late in the day for anyone else to be there. No one but the nurses heard it.

They, at least, applauded.

Now, if they would just tell me if this worked. Is my deadly beasty destroyed?

Chapter 8

Left alone at last, Gemma tried to adjust to the abrupt lack of activity. Her apartment seemed an alien place. Unfamiliar. It was difficult to get back to the routine of her real life.

Work was out of the question. She was a free lance writer, but ideas appeared to escape her, like her imagination had dried up while she'd been sick, and would always be a barren landscape from now on.

Besides, there seemed to be something wrong with her eyes; they slipped out of focus, and her vision was continually blurred; parts of the picture had small gaps in it. She could move her eyes, and a space in the image would be missing.

Her hearing also, would come and go. At times, she could hear the people out in the hallway; on other occasions, the world was unusually silent.

Left adrift, waiting for the next contact from the Cancer Center, Gemma did not know whom to turn to. Should she even tell anyone?

She had dreams at night, where her mind seemed on super drive. Her sense of her body was different; it was transparent, so she could see inside: there were twin hearts, three kidneys, one behind the other two, and many unusual organs...yet, she was familiar with their function, as if she'd been trained in the alien anatomy.

Her brain, too, performed at a level never used in the past.

But, it is all a dream; isn't it? It can't be true.

When she looked into the mirror next morning, her outward appearance was the same: short legs, hips more rounded than before, flat belly, slim waist, and she felt...her breasts would always be inadequate. Too small. But on the outside, she was, as usual.

Even the hair atop her head was finally growing back; very short and prickly, a tight mass of blond-white, sticking up, fuzzy and almost...but not quite, curling.

Beneath a short biker's kerchief, Gemma chose to hide this new development, when she did venture out, which was rare, lately.

She kept trying to contact her sister, Bella, but Gemma always got the answering machine, and Bella never returned the calls. By now, Gemma felt more like an orphan; she really had no family.

Let her be a jerk, then; if that's the way she wants it. She was never there for me the whole time this has been happening...I don't really need her, anyway!

Gemma knew Bella was there. Sometimes, the line would be busy. And it was her sister's recorded voice on the message machine...

With her continual lack of energy, Gemma didn't feel like taking a bus across town to visit her sister, to confront her, so, things were left as they were.

A month turned into six weeks. At last, in the mail, Gemma received her final follow-up appointment.

Maybe, they will, at last, tell me they've conquered the Cancer? That the beasty is dead, and I am a survivor...I can go on with my life, again.

****

Loni could feel the excitement in the air. Even here in the gardens, though this harvest wasn't the usual kind, the atmosphere was energized.

Another crop of females was ready, and the first had begun to come through. The arrivals would continue for the better part of the year, but the evidence would be seen, heard, and felt ...even down here among the workers.

It had been years since Loni had seen a woman. Sometimes, in the past, after their arrival, you could see the new ones, walking in the landscaped park area, with their appointed males. Some would yet be normal, not having conceived, others appeared in various stages of motherhood. Most were very beautiful, causing those without partners to be envious; others were of average appearance, and some were downright ugly, but...they were female. To be cared for, and treasured. They were the hope of a future generation.

Then soon, the nurseries would fill up, and from above, in the distance, you could hear joyful, excited laughter, as the babies began to grow.

It was a happy place, beneath the dome, then...for a while.

But next came the purge.

That was the time when they sorted out the young, removing them from their mothers, and ...destroying all those that were female.

Loni remembered those times well; each month his mother had hid him, for years, until he was a youth, full grown.

Even down here in the gardens, the sounds triggered the memories: screams of anguish; the liquid reverberations of their butchering brutality. He could sense the blood lust of the eliminators.

Why? Why must this be done?

A long time ago, Loni had read it from the minds of their leaders.

Centuries previous, they had made it law: No female of the original race would be permitted to live past its first year; all females born after would be killed, for the safety of the male population.

And why? Because, girl babies, as they matured, were far more intelligent than their male companions; also, they aged more slowly, after reaching a certain age, causing them to live ten times as long.

In the beginning, a powerful, jealous man had seen the dangerous probabilities, rebelled ...and instead of working with his gifted population, made certain, there would never be that uneven dominance.

'Breeder females must come from the more primitive race,' they had agreed. And so, the experiments, far away in another place, continued. The results were this yearly harvest.

Mighty physicians came back at this time, from the other side, on leave, choosing, or having already chosen, a partner. Life began all over again...when the intelligent men bred.

But it was never so down in the gardens. The workers were the rejects...there were rarely breeder females for them.

If they only knew what they had placed among the castoffs...the protection they have unwittingly given to one such as me.

Loni remembered how his mother had died. She had hid her talents, from those in control, for many years, after being separated from her son, but when they had finally discovered the smallest inkling of what she could do, she, too, had been put to death. Rather than admit, they had actually created a female like those of old, her existence was erased from the records of their experiments.

Loni had learned a hard lesson by that: it was better to be thought dumb, than to ever let anyone know they had a male of like caliber in their presence. He kept what he could do to himself.

As for the law; there was little he could do about that. Without exposing himself to a death sentence, he could not help anyone. He would wait, until the time was right.

As yet, he was not fond enough of any other to risk his life for them.

Chapter 9

Gemma wanted to skip with joy. She was free! No more chemo; no more radiation; no more stupid doctor's appointments. The tumor in her sinuses was gone!

"We'll have to have a follow up in about three months," the physician had told her. "But, yes, you can go on with your life. Just remember to eat well, get lots of rest...take a holiday..."

That last wasn't even in the background, as far as Gemma was concerned. Though she had some savings, she'd been using them to get by, and slowly, depleting them. It wasn't wise to take a trip or tour.

Besides, she was a coward, frightened to travel alone. She had finally gotten through to Bella, but her sister was like a cold fish, distant, and uncommunicative. She would never consider accompanying Gemma anywhere.

What is it with her? Is she afraid if she gets close again, she'll be responsible for me? Man! She can be so selfish, sometimes!

****

Peering at the film on the viewer, the physician commented to his companion.

"This one has been ripe for some time. How come she hasn't been gathered in before this?"

The other grunted derisively. "Two reasons: first, she was put on hold...she's been claimed."

"All the more reason, she should have been on her way," interrupted the other. "What is the second reason?"

"Smarter than most. All through treatment, she questioned every detail. We had difficulty keeping ahead of her. Now, she fails to fall for the usual methods we use to draw them in..."

"Well...give her a free trip..."

"We have been trying. She always hangs up on the recorded message; won't let it play long enough to get the subliminal message."

"Do we have to stage another kidnapping? Put the message at the beginning...if that doesn't work, send someone in to her apartment to set up a tape to sleep-suggest!"

"We'll find a way, sir."

"You had better. If she is already selected, she needs to be brought in."

"Right! I'm on it."

****

"Hello!" the bright voice on the other end of the line proclaimed. "This is Amie, and I'd like to award you a free trip to the Bahamas. All you have to do..."

Disgusted, Gemma hung up before the sentence finished. She knew the recording was a scam call, and she was getting more than annoyed. These were the only kind of messages she seemed to get, lately.

Wouldn't it be nice, to really win something...

But everyone in the modern world knew that telemarketers were a scam.

Those born in the country had long ago noticed a certain attitude toward them in the many arriving from the less privileged third world. These new peoples viewed the government, with their numerous subsidies, and health benefits, as their personal cash cow. In their eyes, those born here were naive, and gullible, with more privilege and affluence than they deserved.

Upon their arrival, feeling it was now their right to exploit them, they daringly set up unregistered companies, based back in their homeland, to prey upon the unsuspecting elderly and lower class citizens; thus was the bases of most scams; it was their way to get access to your computer; a way into your personal financial records.

What Gemma couldn't figure, was what benefit it did them, when she didn't bite.

The callers were under the assumption most people were loaded with cash; and expected these would easily fall for the ploy. But Gemma felt, along with her luck, her money tree had failed to materialize; had in fact, died a long time ago. Her EBooks made little money, just a couple dollars at a time. Most readers preferred to download her books when they were up for free.

Gemma assumed this scam was like all the others. Nothing was ever free.

But, now that she had a clean bill of health, she was just mad enough at Bella, for her neglect and abandonment, to take off on that holiday vocation, and blow all her savings to do it.

If I disappeared for a while, it might scare her but good!

The more she thought about it, a trip sounded so nice. To get away from it all, leave her sister behind, not even tell her she was going.

But not a trip to a foreign land. Maybe a tour...to Hawaii.

****

Having finally made a decision, Gemma went on line to find the perfect holiday. There was one, a tour of the Hawaiian Islands' gardens, that she would give most anything to see, and it also, wasn't that bad for price. The costly part was the airfare to get across country to connect with the cruise ship.

Apparently, there was no direct scheduled route. One had to back track, all the way from the center of the country to the opposite coast, then fly back the other way again from east to west.

How stupid is that?

Gemma didn't like it much, but what could you do? It was the way things were.

She booked passage on the cruise, and the flight east, plus the one west across country; paid for the tickets, hoping all the while the two airlines would connect, as they were supposed to. If they didn't, it would put her in a real bind.

When the day of departure arrived, her worse fears were materialized. Nothing went as planned.

It seldom does.

****

The flight from the prairies was uneventful, but upon arrival at the large eastern international airport, the passengers of Gemma's flight were informed their connection would be delayed; it was having engine trouble, the plane was grounded, the flight cancelled. All passengers would be on standby until further notice.

I have ten hours before the boat leaves...it might still be okay.

Gemma could not return home, so like many others, she remained in the airport, hopeful of a quick resolve. The hours passed, while many sought rest in the chairs at their disposal.

Gemma had purchased a prepaid credit card for the tour, but to use it for food in the terminal would make it near impossible to enjoy any future entertainment, so she went without lunch, and then...supper, all in the hopes, this would soon end.

Eight hours later, she was no longer reassured.

"Are you the folks waiting on standby?" asked a uniformed attendant, coming up beside Gemma.

A number of people, slouching, half asleep, came to abrupt attention, at her words.

"We have a plane leaving in twenty minutes; everything is loaded, and you've already been through customs...you just have to get to terminal six, across the building, before they take off. Follow me..."

Twenty minutes was not much time to cover all that distance, but the woman seemed to think it possible. She took off, with a long line of followers, so fast, Gemma nearly got left behind.

Annoyingly, Gemma's vision picked that moment to go defective. The scenes all around her became mostly blurred...a strange place; always unfamiliar, at best. But Gemma was used to this happening, and had long ago learned to find other ways to feel her way through. She could see enough, just to guide her.

She pinpointed a chunky, short, middle aged man, just in front of her, latched on with determination to follow him as closely as possible. He and his wife had been the last to join the group in the waiting room. It seemed, they had just hurried through security prior to their arrival, and the man was still trying to replace articles removed during the search. He lagged, falling back more by the minute, attempting, as he ran, to return his shoes to his feet.

Gemma didn't realize, he'd been unable to replace his belt, until she watched him for a time. Her line of sight was fixed at his waist, and as he ran, the trousers slid down frighteningly over the nonexistent hips. He'd stop and pull up his pants, then run again for a space, only to have them slide down, over and over.

Gemma looked up, as the intercom announced the last call to their flight, and that was when she lost her guide, altogether.

She stood still, fuming.

I've missed it! Pokey old guy! Why did I even follow him?

Out of the fog around her, another attendant appeared at her side.

"Are you Gemma?"

"Yes!" she declared, relieved.

"The plane is waiting for you. Come with me."

Gemma breathed a sigh; she hadn't realized they kept such good tabs on passengers. But the woman did not take off after those she had been following; they turned about, and went back the way she had come.

"Where are we going?" asked Gemma, puzzled. She was getting her completely lost.

"I know a quick short cut..."

****

The airport, in this section, seemed crawling with foreign, bearded, brown-skinned men. They peered from around corners, and doorways, everywhere, ogling her.

It's only my imagination...

From the corner of her eye, Gemma thought she caught a glimpse of a familiar figure.

Gemma stopped short, turning about abruptly.

I didn't just see Doctor Harmon talking to Doctor Gee back in that doorway, did I?

But, when she looked back, the entryway behind was empty; the two men had either stepped back from view, and vanished, or they had never been there at all.

Man! I sure do need this vacation. I'm seeing the ghosts from my past.

Chapter 10

Gemma had thought she was the last one to board, but half way down, on her right, there were still two vacant seats. She slipped into the window seat, so she could watch the scenery as they took to the air.

While waiting, she scanned the other passengers.

Where is old droopy drawers? Did he and his wife miss the flight?

Glancing at her watch, Gemma was hit with reality. Disgusted, she leaned back dejectedly in her seat. She had just realized, she would never make the connection with her cruise.

All that money wasted! What am I going to do now?

I have no place to stay when I arrive; no relatives on the west coast.

Who do I contact?

This is worse than when they told me I had cancer.

Man! I must be the most unlucky person in the universe!

****

Just before they took off, the stewardess helped the last passenger into the seat beside Gemma; a scrawny, unsteady younger woman.

The new arrival didn't lower into the seat gracefully; she plunked down heavily, as if her limbs were unreliable, almost falling against Gemma. The stewardess fastened her seatbelt for her, then went forward to seat herself before takeoff.

As the plane began to ascend, this new seatmate made an attempt to introduce herself.

"My...name's...Ly...di...a," she stammered.

"Gemma," acknowledged the other.

When she reached out to clasp the proffered hand, Gemma was shaken to the core, experiencing a sudden kaleidoscope of images, as they flooded through her mind.

She gasp, as if her hand was on fire, abruptly letting go. It was like the static shock, when sticking your finger in an electric socket; like being mentally flash burned.

Whoa! What just happened? It seemed like I just saw her whole life pass before my eyes.

But, the younger woman appeared not to have noticed anything amiss. She sat back against her seat, going quiet until the takeoff was over and they had leveled off. Then, with the release of the seatbelts, Lydia turned to Gemma, determined to do her best to carry out a conversation.

And...she seemed inclined to expose her whole past history.

Oh, well. At least, it will take my mind off my own situation.

Lydia revealed, she had a six week old baby daughter, who had been left behind with the husband. In the middle of her pregnancy, the young mother had been diagnosed with a brain tumor, but rather than have her baby harmed by the treatments, Lydia had chosen to delay them until after giving birth.

By then the tumor had spread to cover the top of her head; Lydia was stage four, end stage Cancer. They operated, then went for aggressive, simultaneous Chemo and radiation therapy.

The physicians felt they had been successful. This trip west was to do tests to determine whether further treatments, if any, were necessary.

Wow! No wonder she's so weakened. And I thought I had gone through a lot.

"My tumor," Lydia revealed in apology. "Damaged the cognitive center of my brain. Normally, I can think of what I want to say, but can't get the words past my lips."

"Well, you are doing just fine with me."

"Yeah, that's what's so unusual. It's so easy with you; it's like you anticipate the words I want to say, before I have to say them."

Gemma felt a cold draft run down her spine.

I can't be reading her mind? No way!

"But," continued Lydia, proclaiming optimistically. "I intend to be a survivor. I'll be back to raise my baby soon as these tests are over."

"Way to go, girl! We don't give up. Just hang in there!" Gemma encouraged. "I'm a survivor, too. I just conquered my beastie."

"Really?" Lydia smiled excitedly. "Oh, forgive me. I am so sorry. Here I've been talking all about myself, and not even considering what others might be going through. Were you going on a vacation, to celebrate?"

Gemma sighed in disappointment. "Well...that was my original plan, but...I think the airline has kinda screwed me there. I just realized before we boarded, because of the time difference, my cruise ship is leaving port at just this moment."

"Oh, my. What will you do now?"

"Six months ago," Gemma stated. "I thought I had a death sentence; I couldn't even see how to get through my Chemo treatments. All around me were strangers, foreigners with different colored skin, unfamiliar belief systems, some with no belief at all. I realized, the only way I could survive was if I believed there was a personal God, a higher Power in control, and that He would do what's best for me. My maker got me through all that, even healed me...I'm sure, He'll help me through this one, too."

"Oh golly, I wish I had your faith..."

****

While they had been talking, the drone of the engines had changed in pitch. Gemma could feel it, a shift in position, as if the plane was turning or losing altitude, or even both.

From two seats forward, a woman passenger began to irately address no one in particular.

"What the heck is that stupid pilot doing? We are not suppose to be going over water. He just turned the plane, and we are heading out across the ocean. What on earth does he think he's doing?"

Even the stewardess stood up to look. All over the plane, passengers in the aisle seats leaned over to peer out the windows. Gemma didn't need to do that; she had a window seat.

Sure enough, it was true, they were now way out over water with no land in sight. The original plan was they were to cross over the middle landlocked provinces to get to the west coast.

Is the man asleep...or drunk? Did he put us on auto pilot?

This whole experience was beginning to take on the feel of unreality, like a dream sequence gone wrong.

Maybe, I am still in the hospital? I'm in a coma, and this is something my own imagination has conjured up.

Or maybe, I just dozed off in the airport terminal, while we were waiting for standby?

The other passengers were now considerably upset, so the stewardess went forward to pound on the cockpit door, to find out what was really going on. After considerable time with no answer, she sought out help to push the door open.

It was then Gemma realized, all the passengers were women; and there were no male attendants either.

The heavy door was finally forced in...to reveal an empty cockpit. The plane was indeed on auto pilot, flying on its own.

Where is it going?

The pilot and co-pilot had been there at the beginning, and both had been male. When had they left the plane? And without being noticed...how?

"We've been hijacked!" one of the other women cried out with a panicked voice.

At the imagined implications, Gemma's heart began to pound; bile crawled up her throat, as the visions of being in terrorist's hands, hit home. She knew, once again, she was in a helpless situation where there was nothing she could do.

Her mind went blank; she couldn't even think up a decent prayer.

Oh, God...are you there?

And suddenly, a calming reassurance flooded over her spirit; peace from...somewhere. She sat back against her seat, appearing calm and collected.

"How can you be so unconcerned?" demanded Lydia. "Think of those who love us..."

"I doubt anyone will even notice I'm gone," Gemma declared bitterly, thinking of Bella. "My sister didn't even care enough to visit me in hospital. No one will realize I'm lost."

Only seconds later, while still in midair, the engines cut out. The nose of the plane started for the water. Screams immediately filled the confined space.

Her heart was in her throat. Gemma held her breath, as if doing that would give her more minutes to survive.

Lydia began to sob quietly.

"My poor baby," she moaned. "And my husband. He's been so faithful all through this; at my side constantly. He wanted to come along, but I insisted that I'd be alright. He will be so devastated; he'll blame himself. Oh, oh! I'll never see either of them again."

Gemma breathed in deeply, to calm her own rising trepidation. She had always had an unreasoning fear of drowning in water.

Defying her own inner turmoil, calmly, Gemma reached over to fasten Lydia's seatbelt, and after that her own. Then covering the younger woman's hands, which were clasped tightly in her lap, she squeezed to reassure her.

But, that only brought on the shakes. The woman's whole body convulsed as her sobs increased. Lydia grabbed at the offered lifeline, and like creatures buried alive would hang to a saving root, the two clutched hands until this should be over.

Chapter 11

The plane now sat on the surface of the water. Gemma could hear it gurgle as it settled.

Water inched over the wings...

Inside, the passengers waited in silence, their screams choked off in their throats, as resignation to their fate took over. Gemma felt numbness spread from fingers and toes, to elbows and knees, as her pounding heart continued a staccato drum roll.

The nose of the plane was the first to go under; slowly, inch by inch, the liquid rose to the windows.

Foolishly, Gemma expected the intercom to bark out orders for them to evacuate.

They are just going to let us drown?

Water crawled up the windows, shutting away the sky; covering them; submerging them. As if in slow motion, the aircraft slowly slipped beneath the sea, going down, down, ever deeper, gliding as if descending on an invisible landing strip.

Gemma could barely hold back her panic. Beside her, Lydia had fainted, yet even in her unconscious state, she clung to Gemma's hand, as if her life depended upon the junction between them.

A tear escaped the corner of Gemma's eye; her sight was going fuzzy, as if the terror she was experiencing connected to the visual. Hyperventilating, she knew she could not hold out much longer.

Submerged in the silent water, they floated lower, gliding down, as if directed in a planned landing. The bottom clunked against the seabed. Settling down on the sandy bottom, the plane creaked, gurgled. The sound of rushing water filled the confined space.

Oh, God. Oh, God...be kindhearted to us...

Gemma's panicked heart seemed to stand still; her mind drifted away in a fog of denial. Finally, mercifully, she joined Lydia, and the rest of the passengers, in the land of oblivion.

****

Distantly, Gemma became aware of movement at her side; someone had released her seatbelt; was forcing her to stand. There were men all around them, urging them toward the exit.

Lydia was already gone.

At the doorway, an accordion-like, gray plastic, tunnel was attached to the frame. As they followed along this, you could hear the slopping of the water outside, feel the sway of the flexible tubing, as they traversed it, but most of the women were presently beyond fear, living only in a haze of unreality.

Definitely of that condition, Gemma followed orders without question, not even aware of the appearance of the men moving beside them.

****

They passed into an enormous, underwater dome; Gemma could see the metal rafters miles above them, as they were forced forward along a trail below.

It was like a huge airport terminal, a way station, or landing area, where many were milling about, as if awaiting to go to their next destination.

She could see horizontal balconies, with guard rails, above, all around the large struts of the dome. These were crowded with brown skinned people, all men, with black hair and beards, dark eyes and angry features, who gawked at the women, as if appraising them like cattle.

Sprinkled among these were men of a different appearance. They seemed to be servants, carrying parcels, and packages; pairs of them toting trunks between them. Their skin was of a pale blue-white, the hair atop their heads, short; a nappy, tightly curled dark gray. But their eyes were the feature that most caught your attention. They glowed out of the darkness at you, the whites a barely discernable mauve hue; the irises either blue or greenish.

And all of them watched the women below, as if they were something to be devoured.

Gemma shivered, feeling on display, an unwelcome intruder.

Why, it doesn't feel any different than back home! What is this place? Who are these men?

For the next twenty minutes, they inched forward along the pathway, one person at a time, until finally, each came to a doorway. Forced to enter separately, each woman found herself in a much smaller closet-like room.

The chamber contained but one piece of furniture. Standing next to the opposite wall was a mirror-like, lighted, archway, glowing brightly. You could not see through to the back of it.

One man stood next to this. In his hand he held a device similar to a card reader. Stepping forward, he ran it over Gemma's body, then ordered her to pass through the portal.

She was immediately hesitant.

Gemma was in no way unfamiliar with the imaginary teleportation devices from the science fiction movies. She had watched many an episode on the space channel.

Surely, he doesn't expect me to believe this is real? Maybe, this is all a nightmare? Or I'm hallucinating.

"Step through!" gruffly ordered the impatient attendant, and then...he pushed her into the light.

****

It seemed to be only seconds, and she was on the other side; the place, a carbon copy of the first.

But that brief glimpse was all that she saw. Her heart began to do funny dances; her vision fogged, then faded, yet still, as if from a distance, Gemma was aware of men's voices.

"Bah!" exclaimed a startled voice. "Catch her!"

Hands grabbed at her, roughly carrying her.

"This one didn't take to the transfer well..."

"Sit her against the wall, out of the way for now, until she comes out of it."

Gemma did her best to take deep breaths. The effort slowed her heart rate, and the confusion cleared from her mind; her vision started to return.

After a few minutes, she became aware of a shadow standing over her. Once again, she heard the beeping of a hand held device.

What is this? Do I have an identity chip on my body, that tells them I belong here, or what?

"Get up, now!" ordered the man.

Gemma was led away to join the others in a huge holding room.

In the milling crowd of women, Gemma searched unsuccessfully for Lydia. The woman seemed to have vanished.

There were many women here, a lot more than had been on the plane that had descended into the sea. Who knew from where they had all been gathered? They sought answers from each other, and from the silent male guards, but no one knew anything, and their overseers gave no clue.

It was obvious, these men were not their rescuers.

What do you want with us? Why are you doing this?

Chapter 12

When they were at last spoken to, one stepped forth as leader, and addressed them. It was explained, they must strip of all garments, jewelry, anything that would identify them. These would be jettisoned out on the surface of the water, along with pieces of an old, damaged cargo plane, to sidetrack authorities, as they looked for the missing passengers.

For bodies, they had pieces: limbs, hair particles...old dead useless females, and aborted infants.

Gemma shuddered at the cold way the man expressed this last, and visions of their future ran rampant in her mind.

What kind of heartless society have we fallen into? Are these men, human? How can they have existed under our seas, and the governments not known of them?

With the other women, Gemma now stood buff naked, her arms hugging her chest in embarrassment of her small inadequate bosom. There was no use trying to hide anything else. A person only had two hands. She waited in one of four lines; obviously...to be examined.

Leering guards stood on either side of each escape exit, to prevent any female from fleeing.

At the head of each row, was an examining stool; beside each stood consoles, supporting what appeared to be computer monitors. Two men worked each examining station; the attending assistants held handhelds similar to those used back in entry; Gemma couldn't yet see what the Physician's were doing.

Gemma was not merely cold, but trembling from lack of nourishment. She had forgone her meals all the day before, in the airport terminal, and on the plane, water and food had been the last thing on anyone's mind. Nowhere in this huge building, had she seen anything resembling sustenance, and in all the time they had been here, none had been offered. Obviously, these men had no thought to supplying any needs but their own.

As Gemma finally came up to the front, she was considerably relieved and grateful to climb up on the stool to be assessed. Her limbs felt unsteady; her breathing was shallow, and she was near fainting, yet still, she attempted to cover herself, as best she could.

"Drop your arms," growled the attendant.

Gemma obeyed, and he outright laughed.

"Hey," he yelled to his counterpart in the aisle behind them. "I thought we were bringing in cows, not sows?"

The attendant from the next line glanced over, grinned, and shrugged.

"She only has two," he pointed out.

"She'll be useless at feeding," commented Gemma's attendant in disgust. "Too small."

From the stool in the next line, the woman sitting there, started to laugh as she caught on to what the men were talking about.

"Runny eggs," she agreed. "Like having nothing."

Both the attendants began laughing uproariously. Gemma felt her face heat. Surely, she must have gone as red as a beet.

Gemma looked over to the next row, at the obnoxious woman seated on the stool. Naked, the woman sat proud as a peacock, her chest out, the fullness of her girls, riding on her fat knees.

Thanks so much for coming to my defense! At least, I will never be just a sex object, as you are.

Humiliated, Gemma squeezed shut her eyes to prevent the flow of tears that threatened. Yet still, it did not shut away the vision of the ugly, obese creature sitting behind, grinning. As she listened to the raucous laughter of the men, Gemma grew angry.

Why do men always find her kind so attractive? She wouldn't be so pretty if those nipples were festering and sore...dripping blood...

In her mind, Gemma envisioned the other woman's dark flesh points begin to ooze.

"Hey!" exclaimed the startled attendant in the next row. "What's happening here? You're bleeding..."

Appalled by the coincidence, Gemma began to tremble.

Did I do that? How could I?

At a man's touch to the side of her temple, Gemma started violently. Her eyes flew open in shock.

But, it was only the physician beside her, applying small plastic tabs to her person: one beside each eye, another behind each ear, several down her chest, and one in each arm pit.

It wasn't that the tags were uncomfortable. Gemma had endured this procedure many times before; they were just leads for the heart monitor machine.

It was what happened each time the man touched her, that threw her so off balance: a rapid fire of images and suggestions assaulted her senses every time he made contact.

Now, instead of being simply exhausted and famished, Gemma became nauseous, feeling as if on a roller coaster, dizzy and sick.

The man beside her grunted in disgust; he was peering closely at the monitor beside them.

"Oh! Heck!"

"What?" asked his attendant.

"I think, this one is flawed," the physician answered. "And in more than one way. I am certain, she can neither hear nor see."

I can hear you! Your instruments are the ones faulty.

Sure, sometimes I have trouble with my sight, but I know I can hear! And see...better than you realize...

From the other aisle, that physician cautioned.

"You'd best use wisdom, and not reject her. We need every female we can get. A lot has gone into each..."

The other growled at him in anger.

"Do you think I don't know that? This one is already chosen, but...I must still recommend further testing. Her readings are abnormal...she is handicapped."

"She'd still be good to breed?"

What is this? You are not touching me! I'm not some animal!

"Of course, but...she'd bring forth a flawed fetus...a replicate of herself."

The other shook his head.

"What is the matter with the lab physicians, on the other side, that they don't pick up on this, before sending her over?"

"I have to report it," insisted the first. "If her claimant still desires her..."

"He's an old one; been in the field a long time," interjected the attendant.

"I need to go by the rules..."

"Your choice," agreed the physician from the other aisle.

While this conversation had continued, Gemma became more and more puzzled.

Why is no one reacting?

Those around them, all the nearby women waiting to be processed; the other attendants, each appeared either not to understand or hear, or they were ignoring what was being said.

Why?

It dawned on her then: the two physicians had been conversing in a different tongue, and...Gemma had understood every word.

I must be reading them...I don't need to be taught their language!

I'm not flawed! I'm exceptional! But...maybe, that's not good. Maybe, that's what they mean by flawed...

I'd better watch it...

I wonder what they do with someone like me?

And then Gemma knew...without being told.

They would kill her!

Chapter 13

Gemma was sure her poor stomach had given up hope of ever being fed. When she felt anything at all, there was this lethargic numbness; and an empty acid burn, as if her insides were eating at her back bone.

She couldn't stop trembling. The chill of the air on her exposed skin, combined with her fatigue, was getting the best of her, and all she wanted was to lay down, curl up under a blanket, and sleep for a week.

But that wasn't the least of her problems. Every time she came near another person, bumped up against a woman, or even stood near them, images from that individual's memories flashed through her mind. No matter how Gemma fought to reject them, she was bombarded from all sides with rapid fire pictures, like a movie from a past, she neither wanted to see, nor had experienced.

The processing over, the women were thrown together in groups of thirty, in small holding rooms. A large mat was spread on the floor, but no other warm coverings were available. The other women in Gemma's room huddled together for warmth, comforting one another, but Gemma fled quickly to the farthest corner, away from all the rest. There, she sat, hugging herself, knees pulled up, trying her best to make sense of it all, and to warm her very exposed and naked form.

Why are none of the others seeing visions? Don't they hear the thoughts of the men? Am I the only one? I...

Turned out a freak?

Maybe, I'm going totally mad?

Severely traumatized in the first place, at being thrown into this appalling place, Gemma shivered and trembled, feeling very much alone. Deliberately remaining apart, she tried to decide what her options were. It was when she calmed in this way, that she was finally able to sort out the facts she had gathered.

By organizing the images from the men, she knew things...realizations that made her livid with anger; both humiliated and disgusted.

She had never had cancer! They had simply used a tag, and it had gotten infected. But, the brand had originally meant, they had chosen her for their experiments, to manipulate her body and change it, so it would be more like they wanted it.

These obnoxious men had wanted her as a breeder, and it didn't matter that she already was married. Because Sam was in the way, he needed to be eliminated. They had actually stimulated the dormant cancer gene, that is found in every human being, and produced a fast growing tumor in his colon. Even before Sam was gone, they had implanted the chip to keep track of her.

But, somehow, for ten years, they had lost her. Perhaps, because she had immediately moved out of the area. If the infection hadn't gotten bad enough to affect her eyes, they would never have found her again.

It was that fateful recapture that had done her in.

With the DNA riding on a cancer cell, using Chemo and radiation, they had done their best to kill everything relevant to her original humanity.

That foreign matter must take hold!

What kind of sick scientist would be party to such experiments? Is it all to create their super race?

But something went wrong, again, didn't it?

Why am I so different from the other women? Obviously, they cannot hear the lascivious thoughts of these perverted men. I am the only one seeing visions. Why?

Not even the minds of the physicians seemed to have the answer to that.

At least, as long as she didn't touch; she didn't see. That was a comfort. Her head had finally stopped its violent kaleidoscope of sights and sounds.

Gemma sighed in extreme fatigue. Exhausted, she at last slipped away in asleep.

****

Gemma jerked awake. The feeling of being watched was over powering.

While she slept, the room had emptied, and she appeared to be the only one left in it. The wall opposite was covered by a large window, like a viewing room of a pet store. It was here Gemma found men peering in at her.

Am I hallucinating? That can't be Doctor Harmon, and Doctor Gee, again?

And why not? Doctor Gee always did give me the creeps. I knew he was a weird one, right from the first. The old perverted...

But...Doctor Harmon? He always seemed so kind and gentle. Man! Am I ever a misjudge of character. I'll never trust another man again!

Go away, you pigs! How dare you do this to me! I'm not some animal!

The two turned away, as a third man came up to talk to them. Even through the glass, she could hear every word.

"She is definitely flawed," the newcomer confirmed. "Sightless...the eyes were damaged by the infection. I believe, she is, also, considerably deaf, due to another infection in the ears, probably missed during radiation..."

Yeah, whose fault is that? Doc Gee would never listen.

"But, she still, actually, could make a good breeder..."

"Not where I'm concerned!" growled Doctor Gee. "I'll not mate to something defective! I've waited too long to be cheated. Put her down!"

"After all the work that's gone into her? Do you not want the final reward: a life free of labor; one of luxury...waited on, and cared for all your remaining days? You would be one of the governing body..."

"If the offspring were flawed, I would get none of that! My own life would be forfeited. No! Put the creature out of her misery...or...give her to the next applicant."

The third man turned to Doctor Harmon.

"You were next...do you wish to take the chance?"

Considering for a second, Doctor Harmon finally shook his head.

"She's too small," he decided. "She would not be able to give birth to my large frame young. And, no, I don't think I want a flawed one, either."

"So, you both want her destroyed?" demanded the third man. "What a waste of resources."

Silence fell between them, as the attendant appeared to hope for a reversal. Finally, Doctor Harmon bent a little.

"Give her to the servant workmen. At least, she'll serve some purpose there."

"Do you realize, she will be passed from one to the other?"

"Not if one is found compatible...and he chooses to protect her."

The overseer shook his head in discouragement.

"Neither of the two will live long; it will be a free-for-all."

"It is more merciful than out right killing her," Harmon disagreed. "We have made her like us; she cannot be returned to the life she had."

"As you wish," the third reluctantly agreed, and all three turned to walk away.

They had decided her future, with little compassion, or thought to her opinion in the matter. Gemma did her best to hide the tears forming behind her eyes. She would not let them see her cry.

I never asked for this; who made you gods?

Maybe, this is all a nightmare...

Or, perhaps, I am dead...and, this is hell?

Chapter 14

Gemma curled up despondently in her corner. She wondered, if now that she was rejected, would they even give her care? Food had long since been forgotten; her tongue clung to the roof of her mouth for lack of moisture, and her shivering, from the cold temperature, was constant. She closed her eyes, in the hope sleep would make things easier.

Many hours later she was jarred awake by the slamming of the door; they had shoved someone else into the room. It took a minute before she realized, it was her one, and only friend, Lydia.

So glad to see her new friend, Gemma forgot the usual result that touching brought about, as both ran to embrace the other, without a second thought.

But the contact was not as traumatic as might be expected. It was exceedingly comforting: the emotions of relief, the touch of silken skin against cold flesh. Lydia was as naked as a jaybird, her hair like a prickly black brush atop her head, but she was familiar.

The visions, not already known, were of similar mistreatment to that Gemma had endured. And after the initial first bombardment, the emotions of care, compassion, relief, and an almost loving attachment, were welcome, and eagerly embraced by Gemma. It was a blessed gift, to know the other's feelings mirrored her own.

They sank to the mat in each other's arms, cuddling close for warmth, not embarrassed in the least, that they were both female. And...so, they slept, again, to pass the time.

****

Hope never imagined!

They were giving, not one, but two, flawed females to the workmen.

Five had been selected to make their choice. If they were compatible to the one they chose, they would be permitted to mate.

Miracle of miracles, Loni was one of the chosen five. But, Galar also, was one of the other four.

Why are the two of us always put at odds against each other? If they had left me out, there would have been no problem.

As they hurried through the pathway tunnels, not to be left behind, and unaware they were not included, both Scar and Da followed after. The seven arrived breathless at a hallway, where the attendant hushed them. He pointed toward a window.

Peeking in, Loni saw, for the first time, what could be his. You couldn't distinguish much, as the two were sleeping, and intertwined, wound in each other's arms, like puppies, or a pair of abandoned kittens, seeking comfort from each other.

Loni's heart went out to them.

The attendant signaled silence, with a finger to his lips, as Da made a sound of approval deep in his throat. Da imitated the gesture, backing away from the viewing port.

Loni motioned Galar to make his choice, first.

****

Galar felt his whole body tingle. Never before, had feelings remotely like this inhabited his system. So unfamiliar were they, he shivered with anticipation.

I want both of them! But...I can only choose one.

The one with the lumpy chest was too big to get close to; the smaller one would cuddle better.

"I want the boy one; the smaller."

The attendant nodded, sending him out the other side of the hall.

"Scar want the other one," Galar heard his brother say, behind him.

"You can't choose," the attendant whispered, shooing him toward Galar.

"Why not?"

"Oh, let them all choose," came a voice from the room behind Galar. "It'll make it more interesting."

"Fine! I note your choice."

****

The older one appeared to be sheltering the taller female. Loni saw in that a strength of character, so he pointed, that he chose the smaller woman, also.

The attendant nodded.

Da pointed to the larger busted girl. It was accepted, and both were sent into the big room beyond, to await the DNA matching.

The other three to choose, followed, each picking the dark-haired taller woman.

****

"Is it any use to match all their blood types?" quizzed the attendant to the Physician.

The one peering into the microscope, shrugged.

"Safer. If there are offspring, we do want them to be viable."

"Isn't Flaw of a rare blood type?"

"Yes. I'm doing him first." Suddenly, the man chuckled. "Well, lookie here. He matches his chosen."

"You jest! Galar will be livid...he never loses well to the enemy..."

Both men laughed quietly, and the attendant winked.

"I have a suggestion. We never meant for No Name to choose...how about, we just give the second one to him, for the fun of it? See what happens? Nobody cares if they are compatible...we can always abort the fetus."

"Excellent idea! We will do just that, then!"

****

When the results were disclosed, both Galar and Scar turned silent and brooding. The looks they shot Loni, as they were ordered back to their quarters, would have killed a lesser man. Galar hobbled away on his crutch, as slowly as possible, just to make a point. He would get even!

Loni and Da were escorted into a waiting room.

Chapter 15

Gemma was caught roughly by her shoulders, pulled to her feet, and separated from Lydia. Then they were forced from the room, and into a chamber half that size.

Nothing could have prepared her for what came next.

The women were dragged into this room; made to stand against a side wall; punched, kicked and slapped, until they stood up straight, chest out, as if for display; naked and exposed for the men to ogle.

Gemma wondered what was coming next.

Are we going to be raped?

The two burly guards that had accompanied them, moved back to the exit, standing at either side of the doorway, where they waited, as if daring the girls to try to escape.

Shortly, two other men entered from a side room, came and stood against the wall opposite the women.

The younger one was a short, stocky, brown-skinned individual, with dark hair and brown eyes...eyes that told you, something wasn't quite right in his brain. Gemma watched his memories, but they were not only disjointed, but confused, as if he'd not understood what was going on at the time. She noted scenes of near forgotten abuse in childhood; then kindly brotherly care from the man beside him; a garden area, and enjoyed labor tending the plots. Lastly, she felt an appetite that savored everything edible put before him. A simple man...whose greatest pleasure was to eat.

If either of us are given to this one...

He would be good for Lydia...he has a gentle spirit, won't be cruel...

The second man was a little older. He was not dark-skinned as most others were. So different was he, that he stood out, as if he were a lighted candle in a darkened room. Shocked by the sight of him, Gemma felt apprehensive.

He was tall, over six feet, his flesh of a blue-white hue; his body, trim, and well muscled. His hair was cropped close to his head, a tight curly mass of silver-white. Instead of ears, the sides of his face were deeply scarred.

It was as if he blocked his thoughts; she could read nothing from him. That was incredible, since every other man down here came through loud and painfully.

I must have to touch this one.

His eyes glowed out, piercing through you, the whites a pale mauve-white, with irises of bright turquoise-blue. Gemma wasn't certain if that was lust shining back at her...or appreciation. She cringed, shivered, and went to trembling.

He might be slim, but he was taller, and heavier than she...and she had a sense...she was meant for this one.

Why do I have such a fear of a larger man?

I have good reason for alarm with this one! Look at the position I am in...where I am!

****

Loni could not believe how lucky he was. Up close, she was so beautiful!

She could easily fit comfortably beneath his arm, no more than five foot two, a good foot shorter than he. If he didn't know better, he would have believed this was his sister...if he'd had one, or his mother. The resemblance was uncanny.

Her skin was a rosy pink-white. She was petite, but so thin, her ribs were showing. The nipples of her tiny, perfect bosom stood out, extended, as the cold brushed against them; they were delicate, tiny rounds, firm. He felt the need to cup them, gently, and warm them.

Loni's eyes travelled down, but he steeled himself. He would not subject her to the indignant act of studying her belly. The limbs were sturdy, but shapely; the hips, unlike those of a boy, were curvy; the waist narrow, and small. He knew, his hands would almost fit around it.

Embarrassed by the feelings aroused within him, Loni quickly sought her face. On the crown of her head, the hair was gold-white, short and curly. The lips were bow-like; nose narrow, short, like the pictures he'd seen of cupid. But, the eyes drew his shocked attention: blue irises...the pupils...so tiny.

Loni pulled in a breath, realizing...she was physically blind. His heart broke in anguish.

What have they done to you, little one? I will NEVER let them harm you again!

****

The door at the back of the room opened, turning all eyes toward it. In walked an imposing figure. This new personage appeared to be of great importance, perhaps a judge or commander.

All the men in the room immediately came to rigid attention.

The commander moved to a podium, that had been placed at his end. He beckoned for the white-skinned man to come forward before him.

As this one obeyed, the two guards, from the entryway at the back, moved rapidly to Gemma's side. Forcefully, they each caught an arm, pulling her forward before the pedestal, to stand beside the light skinned man.

Her hands were roughly pulled behind her back, and a thin wire rapidly wound about her wrists, binding them together. At first, Gemma tried to struggle against this, but she quickly realized, the wire cut in deeper the more she resisted.

Beside her, the male turned toward what was happening, his face mirroring objection to the rough treatment, but he seemed to think better of interfering, and quickly masked his feelings.

Side by side they stood, the one buff naked; the other fully clothed in a one-piece jumpsuit of blue. Gemma wondered if the stark contrast was meant to symbolize her position where this man was concerned.

Her companion was turned, by one of the guards, until his back was against her own. His hands were then bound to hers, with a silken rope-cord of red.

Gemma tensed as they touched, clenching her fists, resisting with all her being, trying to keep any unbidden images at bay. Surprisingly, there was no assault.

The judge-like overseer spoke.

"You are now bound together. Unless another succeeds in taking her from you, she is yours as mate."

"He cannot read your lips, unless he looks directly at you," interrupted the guard behind them, and he abruptly turned the white-skinned man to face the judge.

The words were repeated.

"Do you understand?"

The man addressed, nodded. The guard undid both their bonds, and the participants were returned to their perspective places opposite each other.

Next Lydia and the short, stocky younger man were put through the same procedure. There was only one difference to the ceremony.

When the words joining them were spoken, the young man was not asked if he understood.

The judge vacated the room; the two guards also left, leaving the exit door wide open behind them.

It was obvious, all were free to go, but...

What happens now?

****

For a minute, Loni and Da just stood there. It had all happened so fast.

Loni read excitement, and confusion in Da's thoughts.

What do I do?

Take her home!

Obediently, Da stepped forward, took the taller girl by the hand, and led her toward the door. As he did so, the older woman, as if anticipating that she was to go with Loni, quickly backed against the wall in fear, inched slowly, as far away from Loni as she was able.

He was fully aware of her alarm, so Loni took on a relaxed stance, waiting, long after Da and his new companion had vanished. The two stood there, eyeing each other, one with apprehension; the other patiently.

The girl trembled visibly. Loni did his best to project the calm exterior that would ease her, but it was hard to maintain. He was both excited, and anxious, himself.

So, he reached into her feelings, to study the woman before him.

Why does she appear so weak and vulnerable?

She was shaking not just from fear...she was exhausted, and...

Starving? Haven't they fed her?

What has been done to her, that she is like this?

Before she could flee, he quickly stepped forward to catch her hand, but he was distracted by a small bluish patch on her left wrist; the upper inner corner was scarred where an IV site had been infected.

As he touched it, his stomach turned with the sudden connection, and, shocked by what he saw, he immediately broke the contact. But he had seen enough: past excruciating agony; pain overwhelming, over periods of time, not just once, but numerous torments.

It made him boil with anger; appalled that this was what had happened.

He took her hand again, and heedless of being an intruder, he travelled forcefully into her memories. There was little she could do to stop him.

All that had been done to change her ran across his mind. He not only saw, but sensed her reactions: the loneliness; the constant pain, the struggles all on her own to cope with the many changes her body was forced to endure. No help at all! No explanation for the why, and the reason...yet she knew...now?

How?

But Loni was more caught up in what had been done to her. And he was exceedingly filled with wrath.

This is how they grow the mates that produce us? How beastly!

Was this done to my mother, also, and she hid this from me?

How can our men be this selfish? Such usury! The animals! They do not deserve to continue our race!

With a shiver of disgust, Loni withdrew abruptly from the female's mind. He gave himself a physical shake, litterly, and stepped back, but was unable to remove completely, the feeling of revulsion from his features.

She turned questioningly to look in his eyes, and the emotion mirrored in her own was of recognizing shocked rejection.

Loni moaned. He had not meant to portray any such thing.

No! It was not you I found offensive.

Had she caught the projected thought?

How do I ease this situation?

****

He seemed so beside himself, Gemma felt inclined to salve his discomfort, so she reached up, curious, to the livid red scar on the side of his face.

Not only did she want to know, why he was so repulsed by her; she wished to know what had caused his disfigurement. He willingly let her in, and it was more disconcerting than she had imagined.

She could see it happening; feel the acid burn through the ear canal, into the nose, and down the throat. Gemma gasped reliving the emotions and feelings.

When a child, she had experienced a similar vision. She had seen a memory, an episode of a childhood friend. Boys had been throwing stones; one had caught her friend on the lip, causing permanent disfigurement for ever after. At the time, Gemma had felt guilty, believing because she remembered it so vividly, she had done the deed herself.

When she had told her mother, her parent had explained it was just a daydream. But, by now, Gemma knew differently. Since coming here, her powers of mental perception had increased tenfold.

And now, other scenes of the man's past were coming through: the cruel tearing away from his kindly mother; his valiant attempts to remain with her...and the horrible fire that had resulted because of his efforts...the reason for his atrocious punishment.

Gemma drew away from him, tears forming unchecked in her eyes. Attempting to close her mind from what she had seen, she sought to erase the disconcerting images. Suddenly, he was helping her to sort, block, and reject the thoughts of others; teaching her. And thirstily, she accepted that instruction.

When again she opened her eyes, he was smiling at her. She could now hear his words in her mind.

You are like me! Were you always a telepath? I learned how, from my mother.

But her thoughts were still somewhat jumbled; she was too overwhelmed to project. Gemma began to tremble uncontrollably, and as he led her away by the hand, her world became hazy from the stress of all that had happened. She never realized, she had gone into a faint.

She was also unaware, when he scooped her into his arms, and carried her unconscious form home.

Chapter 16

She had fallen asleep cradled in his arms, but...when Gemma awoke, both men were gone, and Lydia lay asleep on another mat across the room.

Gemma assumed, she knew what these two men would want, but she was unprepared to give it willingly.

I have to get away from here! I am not property, and I gave no consent.

She reached for a full length garment, folded at the foot of the mat. Her man had put it there the night before, but wouldn't allow her to sleep in the shift. She slipped it over her head now, tied the drawstring belt.

Then slipping off the soft mat, she crawled carefully, silently, on her hands and knees, to the double doors at the side of the room. One part of the portal was barred by a green tree branch, braced from the upper corner diagonally to the opposite lower end. Obviously, it was meant to keep others out, not her in.

There was a door knob on the second side, and Gemma quietly turned this to see if it was locked. It moved, and the door eased open soundlessly. It yawned like a mouth about to swallow her.

Dare I go through?

She peered around the corner. Beyond was what appeared to be a treed in garden space.

No one in sight.

Gemma stood up. Shutting the door quietly behind her, she cautiously slunk away.

In all directions stretched gravel roadways, guarded on either side by enormous evergreens, their trunks ten times the girth around of both her arms extended out together. As far as the eye could see, the pathways went, only dotted in the distance, here and there, by a tool shed, or a ladder fashioned against a wall, leading up into the high lofts above, from which a pale sunlight glow filtered down through the heavy branches.

Up there...maybe? Perhaps, a way out?

For hours, Gemma wandered about, seeking a way out on the ground floor. She met no one; all seemed asleep at this early hour.

The pleasurable scenery she passed through, with the vegetable plots, and treed and flowered landscaped areas, reminded Gemma of her time with Sam. He had built her a small pool with a fountain.

Sam...he made my first dream yard, just after we were married...and these beasts had to kill him!

Tears formed in her eyes. She hadn't thought of Sam in a long, long time, nor had she ever grieved at his loss. He hadn't seemed gone; his spirit always with her.

So much she had lost over the years; the combined defeats flooded over her like a drowning deluge: sorrow; heartache; helplessness; bitterness, and finally overwhelming anger.

What right did they have to do this to us?

Without realizing where she was going, Gemma had climbed as high as she could. The thunder of rushing water came to her ears, and at just that moment, she came out upon a bare girder which formed a bench-like seat over a roaring fall of water. The stream cascaded down at least a thousand feet, to crash into a river-like holding pond, where it was forced between rows and rows of fruit bearing trees.

She caught her breath at the sight before her, backed up, and sat on the natural seat behind. It was then Gemma realized her true position. Here was the very top of the huge dome; she could touch the girders above.

There IS no way out!

Defeated at last, her sorrow resurfaced.

No one was there to see or hear; why care?

And Gemma, at last, wept.

****

Pure terror hit the pit of Loni's stomach; tingles of fear fled through his limbs.

His mat was empty!

Da pushed past him to get in the door, his arms laden with fruit, he'd picked fresh from the trees, to give to his new companion. She still lay asleep where he had left her. The younger man scampered across to the far corner, bounced down on the soft padding, dropping the small, juicy, purple balls, and waking her in the process. Instantly aware Da had brought food, she grabbed for one rolling by, put it to her mouth, and hungrily bit into it. She smiled at her benefactor, the juice running down her chin. Da reached out to hug her, the two falling to the mat with energetic abandonment.

Neither of the pair noticed Loni's shocked, rigid, frozen stance at the door.

I've already lost her! Did Galar take her?

Moaning, Loni moved to his own empty mat, dropped his burden of luscious fruit carefully on the padding. He had selected the produce with such care: the ripest; the firmest; the juiciest.

Her first meal...and, all for nothing.

She had gone away before he could offer it.

Loni sighed; sat down, uncertain what to do.

Where did she go? Why...did she run?

Loni reached out for her mind, but she was nowhere near. He had made the mistake of teaching her to close out other minds, and that included him. They were yet too unfamiliar for her to trust him.

Where are you, little one? Why do you hide from me? I never meant to hurt you.

But the thought struck him:

Did Galar?

Loni went to searching for his adversary; his challenging nemesis. He had never liked looking into the mind of this malevolent boyhood opponent, yet today, he deliberately went in.

And drew back in disappointment. Galar was still asleep. He knew nothing about this.

That means she fled of her own accord. She is fleeing from me...Or did she simply awaken, and go searching for me?

Loni didn't think so. He had seen enough of her thoughts to know she feared him. He would have to win her trust...or die trying.

Catching up a handful of plums, and a peach, Loni filled the pockets of his coveralls, and stood up. Mentally, he reassured Da, that he'd be back soon. Da paid him little mind; he was busy with his new friend.

Loni went out again, determined to find what he had so carelessly lost.

The cameras! The video from them! They will guide me!

For once in his life, Loni did not object to the constant surveillance of the overseers.

But...he could not find her in any of the present live footage. That could only mean one thing. She was the one place where there was no camera...his favorite place to hide when he wanted alone time...far atop the giant waterfall!

****

He found her sobbing uncontrollably. Suddenly, he was beside her, dropping to the bench, slipping his arm about her shoulders, drawing her against him, offering comfort.

It had been such a long time since Gemma had felt a hug, she couldn't resist. Her tears wouldn't stop flowing; her body insisted on shaking erratically, and his shoulder felt so good. She melded into the softness of him, and simply cried.

He waited, patiently, and when finally the moisture came to a slow trickle, he offered her a peach.

Chapter 17

"Why the tears?" he asked. "I never meant you hurt."

"But others of your kind have manhandled and scarred me..."

"I did not..."

She changed the subject. "What is your name? It can't be Flaw, as I've heard them say?"

Loni laughed. "They think I cannot understand...my mother used to call me, Loni. What are you called?"

"Gemma..."

"May I call you, Gem? To me you will always be a gem. I call you that because I see in you a gentle, compassionate, kind spirit."

She made an ugly face, and for a long time was silent. When at last she spoke to his mind, she was attempting an apology.

"I'm not much of a gem right now. I'm bitter, and angry...and want revenge. I am resentful, and I hate all your kind!"

"Believe me when I say, it will do you no good. To hold the past hurts as your weapons will harm only you. I have had much experience in that battle."

Tears formed in her eyes again. He bent forward and gently kissed her forehead. She drew back, as if burned.

"Don't! I never agreed to your stupid ceremony!"

He leaned back once more, and offered reassurance.

"Nor did I...but, I did choose you, out of the pair choice I was given."

She frowned.

"I did not choose the other one..."

"I never wanted to come here! What right do your people have to do these things to us?"

Saddened, he nodded. "No right," he agreed. "No man has the right to subjugate a woman... or anyone, for that matter."

"But they do it! Right here!"

"True. Those that do, are creatures of little morals, and even less intelligence..."

"If you truly feel that way, how can you live with things the way they are? Do you realize the things that are going on?"

Loni had no answer for his ignorance. He of all men should have picked up on this.

"Until now, I did not know," he meekly excused. "Also...it has been engrained in all of us, from an early age, to accept the rule of those who lead us. We know no other way..."

"That's no excuse!" she fired back. "So...now that you do know what is going on, what will you do about it?"

Loni thought a moment.

"I know what I will not do," he declared finally. "I will not be guilty of inflicting my own belief system upon others...if I can influence society for the better, I will do my best to do so."

"Oh...in other words, you'll do nothing, and things will stay the same, until something happens to affect you personally."

Somehow, her words brought him shame. To have her so disapprove of him cut deeply. He dropped his eyes; closed his mind to her, feeling hurt.

"You aren't any different from the people on the land; always at war with those they find different; either eliminate them, or purge the world of their unacceptable view point. And...if they seem inferior, why just keep them out of sight, treat them like animals...don't give them any rights!"

Loni frowned.

She is really angry. Need to turn her thoughts to something more pleasant.

"You and I...maybe, we can be the example...to affect change?"

Gemma sighed. "I'm sorry...you've suffered, too."

****

He took her by the hand, and as they meandered back to his sleep room, Loni detoured past the nurseries, birthing accommodation, and delivery rooms. They were still in the rafters above, where they could see, but not be noticed; hear and watch.

The nursery was a squalling mass of infants in tub-like cradles, men, and some sort of robot, tending them.

"Where are the women? Their mothers?"

"Mother and child are separated shortly after birth. They fear the women will get attached."

"And, why wouldn't they want that?"

Loni attempted to side track her; he knew where she would go with the information.

"My mother and I used to play up here." He motioned to the girders above them, the catwalks running everywhere. "We hid each time they came to separate the babies from their mothers...until I got too big..."

"I saw...what happened," she softly sympathized.

Loni rushed on, to avoid remembering.

"The women are placed in another holding room, fed well...they pump their breasts, so the newborn have milk..."

"Why don't they just let them nurse? Do they even get to hold them?"

Loni shook his head sadly. "Not unless...they can hide with their baby, as my mother did."

"Why!" exploded Gem.

"They want them bred again as soon as possible."

"Pigs!" declared Gemma with disgust. "They are not cattle."

Loni had never thought of it like that. He had always enjoyed the sight of the tiny infants, longed to hold one in his arms. They seemed so helpless at that stage. Now that he looked at it closer...they did belong with the woman who birthed them.

****

Loni realized Gem was fighting back tears. To avoid letting them fall, her eyes went to the roof above them. She swallowed back moisture, and fired a question.

"How come the pressure of the ocean doesn't crush us?"

He looked at her puzzled, unable to hide his confusion.

Whatever is she talking about?

Then he saw the memory in her mind; the entry into their society.

Loni laughed.

"We are not under water. We are only beneath the surface. You must have gone through a jump portal."

"You mean...that door of light?"

He nodded. "I have never seen one, but, yes, that is what it would look like."

"I didn't know we had progressed that far. I thought that was just a theory they were working on. Scientists have actually made a teleportation device?"

Loni shrugged. "How should I know? I am a mere worker drone..."

"Are you a robot? You said, drone."

"I am real; flesh and blood...they are forever taking my blood for..."

He grew silent, as he realized, what they were using his gift for.

But Gem was on another track again, with more questions.

"You have two races in this dome. Can you tell me how that came about?"

Loni shrugged again. "All I know, is my mother told me, she was the only descendant left of the original females of her kind. She said, the world then, was a different place, then it is now..."

"Was she an alien?"

"She was humanoid, same as you, or I. But..." He considered for a moment. "Back then, the men of our peoples feared what their women could do. It seems they had powers...mind powers. To prevent the spreading; what the males considered to be a defect, the women were..."

"...kill what they don't understand!" broke in Gemma with a growl. "Typical!"

Loni sighed. "You really must learn to control your judgmental out bursts. It will get you into trouble..."

"What more can they take from me, eh? They can't blind me, or...deafen me, as they've done you. They can take my life, but right now...it doesn't mean much the way it is."

"Ah, Gem...so bitter. Yet, beneath, when you have worked it all through, you will be a caring woman, again."

She shook her head in disagreement, and he read her private thought:

He has such confidence in me. Wish I could really be the person he sees.

Oh God; what am I becoming.

He gently squeezed her hand, to reassure.

Chapter 18

Entering the door of the sleep-room first, attracted by the ecstatic sounds emanating from the far corner, Gem looked over, and gave a shocked gasp. Da was atop Lydia, both moving in a familiar rhythm she hadn't indulged in for over ten years.

"Oh, gosh," she declared, turning away embarrassed. "They are making love..."

Loni grinned boyishly, and led her to his mat. When seated, she demanded, in a forced whisper.

"Sure didn't take him long. She's married with a baby back home! Do you know that?"

"All Da understands is that she's been given to him. He's an innocent, following his emotions and urges."

"And so, he just forced her?"

"I don't think so. It looks like, she was quite willing..."

The noises from the other side had quieted. The pair lay side-by-side recovering.

"Does he realize, he is being watched?" Gem challenged.

Loni looked up to the ceiling, at the plainly visible video camera, and for the first time, Loni swore. He moved to his feet rapidly, and to the other mat.

"Da," he said in the boy's mind. "Time we went to work."

And Da obeyed without question. Both men brought along their partners.

It was not permitted for anyone to go idle.

****

She noticed, the first empty showers against the wall were spraying constant hot water. Steam filled the large common shower room, and at first, Gemma thought they were alone.

She felt grungy all over from hauling the bags of wood chips to be spread beneath the flowering trees of the landscape. Her hands were filthy; nails black with dirt from the soil of the garden; weeding out the unwanted plants peeking through.

A shower was most welcome! Even if it must be shared in the presence of these two men. After all, they had first come to them, naked as a newborn.

Following Lydia's uninhibited example, Gemma quickly shed her filthy shift.

But, why is Loni so tense?

Even Da acted as if something were wrong; his whole attitude anxious.

It's as if the two expect to have to defend themselves...or fight for the showers.

It was then Gemma became aware, there were others in the shadowed steam. They were coming from all sides, dozens of naked men, creeping upon the four, surrounding them, their minds curious...and lustful.

Gemma shivered.

Loni's mind-voice came through loud and clear, to all three of his companions: "Da, stay in front of the girls. Let them have first turn at the showers. We protect!"

"'kay," Da thought, and obediently moved to shield Lydia.

"Gem, you and Lydia move back under the water. We will keep them from touching you..."

Lydia whimpered fearfully; she had suddenly realized the precariousness of the situation. Gemma put her arm about the younger girl, and led her under the flowing water.

For a second, the women drew in their breath with shock, as the heat scalded over their bare shoulders, but each quickly adapted.

"Soap is on the ledge behind you," offered Loni.

As the sizzling water cascaded over her dirty curls, Gemma was aware of the frustrated grunts of those confronting Da and Loni. Like animals fighting at a feeding trough, the aggressors shoved at Loni, whose mind was as busy as his hands.

Gem watched as he made suggestions, distracting and turning the enemy away, one at a time. Amazingly, the two boys were gaining the upper hand, though outnumbered ten to one.

She kept her shower short. Even the dirt beneath her fingernails, was disposed of rapidly by the driving hot spray.

"There are towels and clean coveralls on a shelf to the right," Loni revealed, anticipating their readiness. "Hurry and dress. Once you are covered, they will lose interest."

Without question, Loni was leader of the group. He seemed to know what to do; they all trusted, and obeyed, without questioning.

"Now, you, Da...take your shower."

Gem shook her head in disgust, wondering:

Is this how it will always be? Fighting for every private moment. How can we live like this?

"It will only be for tonight," Loni answered in thought. "They are already moving away. When you are clothed, the novelty quickly wears off."

But Gem still felt exposed; she wanted this over with, as soon as possible.

"You, go shower," she ordered, taking over. "I saw what you did to keep them at bay. I can implant suggestions, just as you did..."

Loni laughed, delighted. "You learn fast," he marveled, obeying a little reluctantly.

When, at last, they were all clean, Gem gave a relieved sigh. She had never been a public person, especially where bathing was concerned.

On the way back to the men's quarters, they passed an unmanned fruit stand; Loni and Da simply grabbed what they wanted for their supper, and the girls followed suit.

They were all weary enough to head for bed directly after, surrendering immediately to exhausted slumber, each girl cuddled up, backed up into the arms of their partner. There were no objections this night; even from Gemma.

Chapter 19

Loni started awake. He had almost forgotten he had a sleeping companion; it was that comfortable with her.

In his arms, Gem had suddenly gone tense, as if for a second, she had stopped breathing. Now, she was struggling desperately for breath, gasping for great gulps of air, unable to pull them in quickly enough, as if her lungs were paralyzed.

Loni could feel her two hearts pounding out of sync, warring with each other; getting in each other's way. One was beating too slow, while the other, impacted by the first, fought to compensate.

He was next aware of excruciating pain, shooting from shoulder to shoulder, across her back. To add to this agony, the pressure spread across the front to her chest, and up the side of her neck.

From the way she was fighting it, this apparently was not the first time it had happened. She continued to thrash about, fighting the rebellion of her body, until the phenomenon should ease. But, Loni knew, without help, it would not end well. Gem's new hearts were about to cease, altogether.

He had immediately realized what was causing her dilemma: the physicians had failed to bring her second organ into union with its partner, so the two would not be constantly striking together. Perhaps, it had been an oversight, or maybe, purposeful; he couldn't be the judge, but now that she had been placed among the flawed, medical aid would be withheld...unless, it was to prolong a pregnancy.

****

The pain in her chest, and lack of oxygen, had driven Gemma to abrupt consciousness; the awareness of the man at her back, rudely brought to the forefront, as he circled her front with his arms.

She tensed even farther, when his left hand went from beneath her left arm to between her tiny breasts, the fist rising to catch at her right shoulder. With no time, nor energy, to wonder, what he might be doing, his other hand bunched against her back, between her shoulder blades, pushing hard at the knotted muscles there, forcing them to release. It seemed as if his mind was also inside her, affecting the struggling organs within. As her twin hearts began to synchronize, and the pain subside, Gemma realized...Loni was healing her.

That feels sooo good!

Suddenly, their minds were one, and she was watching his every effort. He corrected the beat of the weaker organ, made it stronger, and waited for the other to come into step, then beating together, the pressure became nil.

She gasped with the pleasure of being pain free. But, she felt his exhaustion, from the mind-effort it had taken. As he released her, he cautioned her:

"Don't tell anyone, I can do this. They fear anyone with powers such as these. And if you can do such...it is best to hide the fact."

"But," objected Gem silently, as well. "They already know...they consider me blind and deaf, but I know, I see...in another way."

He agreed, slowly stroking her back to sooth her further.

"They cannot understand how you communicate, but they don't, as yet, realize you are telepathic...we must never let them know the full measure of our gifts. It must remain our secret. Just pretend, as I do, that you don't understand. Make no effort to communicate with them; their intelligence is too limited to comprehend..."

Again, even as he was drifting off into slumber himself, his hand moved gently, soothingly, across her back. The twin organs were beating now, like a great, two-cog, synchronized clock, moving comfortably, one beside the other.

And so, the two slept.

****

Waking in the night, Loni held her carefully against him, as if he thought she might break, were he not careful. Tears formed in his eyes; one travelled down the cheek, to the cotton sheet. He rested his face next to the silken skin of her face, and thought proudly:

My acquired female!

She is more than I have ever hoped for; my treasure! I will never let them take you from me!

His own double heartbeat quickened excitedly; his body tingled with a new found heat, and holding Gemma protectively against him, Loni finally relaxed again, and went back to sleep.

Chapter 20

The next day was a free day. Loni intended to use it to take Gem back above the waterfall.

Da wanted to bring Lydia, and come along, but Loni ordered him to stay in their room.

Of course, Da always obeyed him. But, he too, wanted to play with his mate.

Knowing what Da had in mind, Loni cautioned him to amuse himself under the garden trees, where the surveillance cameras could not see.

Freed up from responsibility, Loni led Gem over the climbing girders to the seat above the falls. He had come prepared, his pockets stuffed with fruit to share.

Gem, enjoying a luscious peach, was just savoring her second bite, when Loni slashed at his arm with a sharp knife. Blood spurted out from the cut.

"Oh, gosh! What are you doing?"

"I want you to heal me."

"Here? Now? Won't they see?"

"No cameras up here."

"Okay." The peach forgotten, for the moment, Gem quickly obeyed, easily closing the wound.

"Now, let me cut you, and...you heal yourself."

"No! The knife hurts. I'll do it another way."

"How?"

Surprised, Loni stared at her.

What other way is there?

An ugly gaping wound appeared on her arm, red blood oozing.

Shocked, Loni gasped. His eyes went wide in horror. He had never thought to reverse the process.

Why would you want to harm yourself...or another?

It dawned upon him then, just how deadly this power was.

Can Gemma be trusted?

"How about you do the healing?" she suggested, knowing his thoughts, but ignoring them. "Since you want to play like this."

He did as she bid, feeling foolish. When it was done, she scolded him.

"I can hurt others, but...I don't want to, Loni...okay? And, we don't have to practice. I've got it."

He nodded; quietly sat there, awaiting her next action. Never before had he dealt with a mind of equal intelligence.

Loni kept his deep thoughts to himself, and somehow, she, too, had learned to cloak her thoughts. So each sat there, private and distant.

So fast, she has caught on.

When, at last, she did project a thought, unexpectedly, it did not concern the subject in question.

"How do I stop this, Loni?" she demanded, vehemently. "How do I end this, so I can go home?"

It both shocked, and saddened him, that she disliked it here with him. His lot was a good one, compared with others; his work station one of the best. He had actually earned his way up to the privileged worker class.

Then, he realized just what she had said: 'go home.'

He remembered the visions of her home: family life non-existent; the hospital stays, and was amazed.

"Why would you want to go back to such a life, with its pain, indifference, and...loneliness?"

"It's familiar, and...I am...free, there!"

He thought on that, for a second.

Free? What does she even mean by that? I have never been as free as now...

While he pondered, and puzzled, she carried her original thought forward.

"And when I get away from here, back to where I belong," she declared, with forcefulness. "I am going to put a stop to all these experiments! I will expose those doing this...even if it costs me my life!"

He frowned; his lips pursed into a straight, hard line. He had never thought of this whole procedure from her side of it.

No wonder she is so angry! It isn't me, as a person, she rejects. Our whole society is offensive in her eyes. And, I don't much blame her...

What the intelligent...the leaders, the physicians, those over us...have done... They invaded, used, conducted tests, without even permission...and, all for our benefit, never theirs. Oh, how, offensive...insulting...degrading. She SHOULD hate us...me?

Beside him, she was reading his unguarded soliloquy with himself. Her attitude softened.

"Show me how to get home, Loni," she pleaded. "Please."

His heart filled with regret; he shook his head.

"I cannot. I don't know how. I couldn't even find the jump portal. No one in this sector has any knowledge of where it is located. I can't read about it from them..."

"And," he added. "Even if you could go through backwards...

"What do you mean?"

"I know this much about such things," Loni admitted. "Our jump portal is programmed to one destination. You can only go that one way, until it is changed by the other side..."

"I can't get home through the light doorway? What about another way?"

"I know of no other way out of here. I would have gone myself, if there was a way."

Her shoulders sagged in despair, the hopes deflating like a great punctured balloon.

"I don't want to stay here, Loni!" she moaned. "This is...a living hell!"

Those great, beautiful, blue eyes filled with moisture. No longer hidden, tears slipped unchecked down her pale cheeks.

At last, surrendering, even though she feared him, Gemma sought solace in the arms of her companion, one so strange in appearance, she viewed him as a creature, not a man.

Little did she realize, she looked exactly like him, now that her change was complete.

****

Carefully, Loni dared to place his arm around her shoulders, pulling her against him. And when the sparks flew...he held on for dear life.

Yes, litterly...sparks flew. She knew his ulterior motive, and she did not want that. Rebellion rose up, hot and static, within her. He not only felt it, but there was the physical evidence.

When it first started, Loni jumped; the shock wave travelling up his arm to his shoulder. But he steeled his resolve against the static electricity, the blue and red visible waves passing through, and over him.

Whoa! I didn't know that was possible. Even mother couldn't do that...or, could she? Maybe, she hid the fact, because I was her son?

What a defense!

If I was any other man, her protection would have killed me.

Loni persisted, consolingly, running a hand up and down her arm, until the phenomenon ceased.

Submitting finally, Gem relaxed, slumped against him; the tears turned first to deep sobs of defeat, then admitted hopelessness...

And sometime, much later, he showed her his love...a comforting, gentle affair she would never forget.

****

In the weeks after, he didn't touch her often. He was not demanding, and she would not ask of him, but many times desires overcame them, and needed fulfillment. Gem preferred privacy; she loathed giving the watchful eyes at the monitors their thrill. Ever after, they made love beneath the trees by the waterfall, where no man could observe.

Chapter 21

The minute Gem stepped through, and the heavy doors fell shut behind them, she was assaulted by the mental noise from the dozens of minds all around her. She did her best to block away the barrage of senseless musing, and succeeded. When she became aware of what the place held, she quickly forgot, they were even there, at all.

There was food everywhere!

Up until this day, Loni and Da had always brought home fruit and beverages, from the stands along their route home, but, as a treat, like going to a restaurant back home, tonight, Loni had suggested going out. It would be Gem and Lydia's first time eating among the other workers.

Da had been whole heartedly enthusiastic, but the two girls had no idea what to expect.

Sometimes, at the fruit stands, other foods then fruit had been available: porridge, pressed roasted wheat cakes, or sweet leftover baked goods. And juice, squeezed from the various fruits, and vegetables, had been obtainable from taps, but...all this was in limited supply, and not often available.

It was common practice to keep their large mugs in their backpacks for the purpose of filling them at these taps; they also drank from the streams along the way on the worksite.

The girls each had been provided a kit upon arrival in the workstation, which included a pack, containing essentials, toiletries, etc; and was for storage of other treasures you might expect to gather in a lifetime. Of course, your most valued possessions were your eating utensils. It was wise to never leave your pack behind, or unattended; the loss of a cup was considered a great handicap, and was not easily replaced.

The room they entered was similar to a school cafeteria: an aisle between two rows of multi-tiered shelves, one on either side, each covered with multiple food choices.

Loni motioned his menagerie into the thick of it. It seemed you were to pass through to tables beyond, where you sat down to eat. Like at the fruit stands, there seemed to be no currency exchanged; you simply chose your favorites.

Da, in the lead, picked up an aluminum tray, and began loading it. The girls followed suit, with Loni taking up the rear.

There was the usual variety of fruits: pears; peaches; apples; oranges; plums; and many Gem had never seen previously. Next there were cakes: the pressed roasted wheat, a rice cake, and maybe...that was oat? Next came beverages: fruit and vegetable; apple, pineapple, grape; carrot, a green kind, and what appeared to be milk.

The new foodstuffs available were fascinating: boiled eggs and fried ham...at least, that was what she thought it was. Next came cut breads, of all shapes, shades, and sizes. They seemed baked in the most primitive manner, as if in an outdoor, sun-powered oven.

Again, there was porridge, but of three separate kinds: wheat, oats...and was that, rice?

Beyond were the heavier dishes: cooked vegetables: carrots and peas; beets; cauliflower and broccoli; and beans of all colors.

Next was some sort of stew.

And then came trays of meat. Gemma couldn't decide what kind it was. In one tray, she thought she saw a finger, another a toe was among a mushy hamburger dish...

Her stomach turned over.

What are we eating here?

Another tray appeared to hold chicken, with feet, beak, and eyes of the bird included.

There were other meats she could not identify, and fish. It seemed most preparations were more raw than cooked. Who knew for how long they had been on display?

****

As they waited behind Da, Loni projected instructions to the women between them:

"Most any vegetable should be okay, but be careful of the meat dishes; if you don't recognize it, don't take it."

"Why?" enquired Gemma. "What are they made of?"

"We recycle everything. When old ones die, they grind them into hamburger...the meat is tough. Oh, and...the milk may also be human..."

He didn't get to complete the thought; both girls were already gagging.

"Cannibals," went through Lydia's mind, and Da laughed outright. He had actually followed their thought conversation.

Loni read the thought that followed:

"The little people...the female babies that are destroyed, are tender."

Disgusted, Loni scolded.

"Don't eat the meat, Da!"

"Okay," he agreed, obediently.

Loni shook his head.

What am I going to do with these guys? And now, I have the two women to look after, too.

****

Having chosen what they wished to eat, the four moved to a corner, where there was a large horseshoe shaped table with a padded bench. Loni directed Gem to go in first. She slid all the way around until she was at the far exit; Da, as always, followed Loni in, with Lydia next to him. So they sat, all four against the wall facing out, in the middle, with a seat free at either end. It wasn't that they wanted company; it just happened...to their later regret.

Normally, such an action would have been safe. No one bothered Loni or Da when alone, but today, with the females with them, all eyes were on them, and curious. Most of the worker males were too shy to approach, but there were two that had no such compunction.

Suddenly, Galar slid in beside Gem, and his twin found a seat next to Lydia, effectively imprisoning everyone else into the bench with no way of escape.

Why did we leave the girls on the outside? How stupid of me!

****

Gemma cringed, and moved closer to Loni, at the sight and feel, of the ugly, smelly man sliding in beside her. He was much like most of the brown-skinned individuals, with his black hair and beard, and soul-less, impenetrable, dark eyes. He was over six feet, with the face of a Neanderthal; huge, unkempt, bushy eyebrows, stooped shoulders, and long, hairy arms; thick chest hair peeking over the top of his coveralls. One other thing was different; he was missing his right leg, and used a crutch, quite deftly, to navigate.

His brother, who moved in beside Lydia, was his spitting image, except he had only a right arm. For the slit second Gemma was connected to their minds, she knew they had once been conjoined twins, separated after birth.

Normally, that would have incited empathy for them in Gem, but they reeked so terrible, their stench took your breath away, and that made it hard to be sympathetic.

Have these guys never bathed?

And then she had the answer: they worked with the cattle.

****

Galar set his crutch under the table, and moved closer to Gem. She cringed in revulsion, and Loni had the great desire to put his arm protectively about her shoulders, but it would only give Galar an excuse to be his usual obnoxious self, and Loni could sense, the man was already perturbed about something.

"You are mine!" Galar declared bluntly, to Gem. "When we picked, I was first. Flaw stole you; tricked them...somehow. When I get the chance, I will steal you back from this moron. Why, he can't even talk to you."

Both Loni and Da knew it was best to disregard these two. The girls picked up on the action, and as Galar was used to such treatment, he soon cooled, and went about devouring the contents on his tray. Neither eating, or being ignored, ever had dampened his desire for conversation, before, and it was no different now; whether he was understood, he did not care; he could as easily talk to himself...or Scar.

"It doesn't matter that the physicians decided to give this woman to you, Flaw. I will win her...and take her, in the end. I doubt you even know what to do with her. Remember... possession is the law..."

Loni felt Gem shiver beside him, and he wanted to slug the crude Galar.

Silence reigned for a moment, while Galar tore roughly with his huge hands, and strong teeth, at the meat on his plate. He wolfed it down like an animal.

From the other end of the table, Lydia decided to get into the conversation, seeking to steer it from its present course; her stutter was extremely evident, attesting to her nervousness.

"How cu...come you only ha...have one arm?" she asked of Scar. "How did you lo...ose it?"

The second twin stopped with a piece of chicken half way to his mouth. "Didn't lose it; never had it."

Galar took up the narrative for his brother, noisily talking with his mouth full.

"We was born together. The physicians used us for an experiment; tried to make two of us. We had only three legs, so Scar got two, and I got one...I got two arms, though, and he got only one."

Galar swallowed a chunk of meat whole, choked and gagged. He went to coughing, and finally, catching his breath, went on again.

"Scar cannot reproduce. I got the goods to do that. They made him a hole, so he sits like a girl, but I got the hose. I am fully functional!" he added, proudly.

Loni was appalled. He had never realized the full scope of the torture inflicted upon the twins. His experience with them was limited to negative interaction; they had always been his bullies, so he'd been reluctant to enter their minds, therefore, he hadn't sought the reasoning behind their behavior.

"Does he...he," stuttered Lydia. "Can...he...get rid of solid...waste?"

"Oh, yeah," Galar agreed, non pulsed. "They gave him a tube, and a hole in the backside, for that."

Scar seemed unconcerned that his private functions were being discussed; simply carried on eating.

Loni felt, for the sake of the girls, even Scar's benefit, he needed to turn the conversation away from this disgusting subject. It wasn't conducive to enjoyable digestion. Gem had barely touched her meal.

Strangely, uncouth Galar, who had finished with his own, noticed her lack of appetite.

"Don't you want that?" he asked, condescendingly. "I'll eat it for you."

But, Gem pulled it close to her, protectively, as if she thought, he might snatch it away, anyway, should she refuse.

Galar took the hint. "Alright, then. Think I'll go get some more. You coming, Scar?"

As if still junctioned, the two rose from either end of the table, and sauntered off with their trays, Galar hobbling on his crutch, his tray balanced expertly in the opposite hand; Scar following, doing the same with his, almost like a whole man, with two arms, and as many trays.

They were no sooner out of sight, then, as with one accord, and of like mind, the two couples rose, and quickly vacated the eating area. They couldn't leave quickly enough to suit any one of the four.

Neither of the two men, Loni or Da, ever was amazed, or puzzled, by the fact, ever after, their mates avoided the cafeteria, as if eating there would bring on the plague.

Chapter 22

Galar soon realized, if he was to accomplish his purpose, he had to get Loni, and his crew, out of their protected status lodgings, and in the open. He had the perfect means to do it, too.

When middle age had hit the twins, they were moved into maintenance, where Galar learned much about the workings of the dome; the waterworks, electrical control, and most of all, the computer controlled by-pass systems running the overall life support. It was here, he planned to strike at his adversary.

Today, he hung by one leg from repair girders, high above the lodging of the garden crews, sawing under the largest water pipeline passing through the area.

He had already programmed the environmental controls; it would take them months to find the glitch that continually messed everything up.

This was his last little detail. Then he was ready to watch his work produce fruit.

He was pleased; on the pipe he was working on, there was, now, not only a film of dampness, but also beads of actual moisture seeping through the cut.

It's enough!

Galar tucked his tool in his belt, inched along the line, until he was over his crutch leaning against the wall. His drop-down was easy, and obviously, of long time practice.

****

Lydia's strident scream woke them all. Gem and Loni sat bolt upright, both peering across at the other pair in the semi darkness of the night-sleep dimness. They assumed

Da had pinched his partner to tease her. But...the sound of rushing water disproved that.

Gem looked at the far-wall rafters above. A cold sheet of impenetrable moisture was litterly rolling in and down, dropping in a shocking deluge, as thick as the main falls, right on Lydia's head.

No wonder, she screamed!

Loni was the quickest to come to his senses, sending out mental instructions.

"Grab your mats, and any belongings...this is something the administrators need to deal with. We'll go to the huge falls, until it's worked out."

They had only to refill their back packs, and shoulder them; then the men took off with the mats on their shoulders. They were away, out the door, quickly. But when the door was opened, they were shocked by the fact, the only water was crawling over the floor behind them. None was in the hall.

Then, they noticed the activity beyond: hurrying workmen, cursing...and the lights were out, sporadically, everywhere.

Rapidly, the four fled into the rafters, and girders leading above and away. An hour later, they had set up a permanent campsite above the huge falls.

Lydia was drenched to the bone, and shivering, and while Da set to comforting, and drying her off, Loni and Gem watch the beehive of activity in the valley below. It seemed, the whole dome system was involved, from basic worker lodging, right up to the infants in the upper rafters.

What could have caused such a disruption?

Loni wondered, if Galar and Scar were somehow involved? The deed had their markings all over it.

The strangest thing, also was, little of the water system was affected, save for Loni's quarters, and...life support, fire rescue, policing, and certain security, along with anything automated, and under computer control.

Loni and Gem easily listened in by mind, as the workmen talked back and forth.

They spent a pleasant night camping out, but the next day, work stations were back to normal; even the fruit stands were manned, and the showers and cafeteria, ran smoothly.

It was as if the four had not been displaced; as if nothing had happened to the installation. The only difference was they were no longer controlled by the machines, and...some services, such as supervision, was unavailable.

Yet, most carried on as if they were still being overseen; habits being hard to break.

Ever after, all over the dome, breakdowns and failures plagued future operations.

As for Loni, Da, and their companions...they were never appointed another sleep room; perhaps, no one realized, theirs had been damaged.

One man did, and he was very pleased with the situation...

Chapter 23

Gem let out a startled squeak, as Galar dropped suspended upside-down from the scaffolding above, into the pathway. She hadn't been paying full attention to her surroundings; thinking she was safe, so used to the free open spaces of their camp, she had forgotten, someone still might mean her harm.

Loni, too had become lax, figuring she could take care of herself; after all, Gem could defend herself against him. Why not another?

It was their practice to meet up at the falls after work; today Loni had offered to pick up the food; had suggested, the girls take their time with their showers.

They still had to be careful of the other men, but the two women stayed together, so Gem could protect Lydia. Da's woman had ran on ahead...

Apparently, Galar had waited until she had passed by.

The man reached down for her with determined aggression. Gem felt, he was of little threat, suspended like that; there would be no need to zap him.

She sidestepped, and ran past him, into a side path of the gardens. It was just a matter of getting to the other wall, and the ladder leading up. Galar should take considerable time to get operational with his crutch.

But when she reached her goal, the other brother, Scar, was there to meet her.

Bummer! They are working as a pair. Harder to avoid.

Gem didn't dare call out for help; that might bring attention of other workers to her, and when they realized she was alone, they would sooner help the twins then defend her.

She turned down another roadway, heading for the opposite wall-ladder up, but once again Scar had anticipated her. As they headed her off, she got further and further away from the upper campsite. It was as if the two men were guiding her, just where they wanted her to go.

****

"Hey!" shouted a man at the monitor over in the corner. "Come take a look at my screen. Isn't this Flaw's appointed she?"

"Yes. Why? Whoa!" the other added quickly, as he bent to peer at the second viewer. "He's about to lose her to another..."

"What's that?" asked a third, from over the way, standing up, and leaving his post. Soon every observer was craning from behind to see; none were at their posts.

Discipline had been slack ever since the day of the breakdown, seldom being enforced.

"Oh, darn!" They've gone under the trees. This is the pits! We've simply got to put up more cameras in the work areas."

"Yeah, there are none in the butchery, either, and that's probably where they are heading. That's where the twins will catch the little she devil, too. They know the area best."

"Where is Flaw? I don't see him anywhere."

"He's never been in the picture."

"Well, we can't see much more, unless they move back this way, best get back to work," suggested the supervisor. "Let Flaw fight his own battles."

As they returned to their stations, the men were laughing.

"Too, bad," said one. "They made such a good pair. Tough luck, Flaw.""

Howls of laughter, and crude remarks followed.

"Would have been nice to have watched it, though; like a fight match entertainment..."

The incident was soon forgotten, and rumor the next day, gave no inkling of whom had won out.

****

Gem had made it to an up-going ladder, but as she stepped up on the first rung, Scar caught her rapidly from behind. He grabbed her by the hair, and shook her angrily; clearly perturbed by her constant evasion.

The interval was just long enough for Galar to catch up. He came from behind, slugging her from the side, with a heavy branch.

Stunned, the girl went down.

Distantly, Gem could hear, as Galar said: "I'll take it from here; you stay away, now, so he doesn't find us."

The world receded. Gem felt herself dragged by her hair, along the metal hallway, heard the screaming of a door-hinge; then awareness faded away completely.

****

When she came to, her head pounded with a throbbing headache, one like she'd never experienced before. It was so overwhelming, she couldn't even transmit thoughts to Loni, to tell him where she was.

But, he will find me! He won't just leave me here with this brute!

She found, she was also bound in chains, inside a dark, hot room with aluminum walls, and a heavy, iron, padlocked door. Air from a vent, high above, could be felt. But oh, the odors coming through did not alleviate the situation.

Gemma gagged, and retched. To the stench of decaying, butchered meat, and defecation, the contents of her stomach was now added to the mix.

Gemma groaned in misery, wiping at her mouth.

Apparently, having heard her, Galar realized she was conscious, for a rattling at the door told her, he was undoing the lock.

The screech of the door hinge, and dim light entered the rectangular opening. Galar stepped into the room, and switched on a glaring overhead light, blinding her.

Gemma screamed angrily at him, and with her mind, willed him severe pain in his gut, but it was ineffective. Something was wrong. Somehow, the man had blanketed the room with an unknown EM frequency that made it impossible for her to use any mental weaponry.

She could feel the charge now that the door was open. It made her head buzz, and body vibrate, making it tingle.

He seemed as unaware of the effect of his block, as of her angry screams. Gemma went quiet.

"Here's how this is going to work," Galar's hollow voice echoed from behind the glaring light. "I captured you; you now belong to me."

That is quite obvious. But how the devil did you know about my abilities; Loni and I have never done anything when others are around? Did this EM frequency just freakishly happen? He's not that smart. Is he?

"You obey me, or..." he went on. "Or...you stay in here until you agree. You help me, are my mate...after I've let you out..."

He paused, as if waiting for an answer. Gem decided to wait him out, so remained silent.

"Just so you understand the full scope of things. I have reprogrammed the entire dome system differently. I have eliminated all supervision, and policing. They no longer have control. Outside my work station, I have created a static barrier. It keeps everyone out I don't want in here, until...you submit to my way of doing things...according to my satisfaction. And this is how I want it: you will serve me, help me with my work, eat what I give you; no complaints. If you fight me, the barrier stays up, until...I feel I can trust you...to stay with me, and only me!"

This guy is living nuts! There is no way he knows what he's done to me, how he's handicapped me, but I can't do anything about it, until I can get him to trust me. Maybe, Loni can do something from outside...Until then, guess I have to play along.

"And don't expect Flaw to rescue you. He's already tried a number of times. He can't get through my barrier. It repels him."

Great! That means it works against Loni, too. It must be similar to the shield I zapped him with when we first came together.

"And, in case that isn't incentive enough. If you don't say yes, now, you'll stay in here for days...It doesn't matter to me if you die. If I can't have you, he won't have you either. You keep up your rebellion, and I'll outright kill Flaw. Enough voltage will fry him good."

At that point, the buds of hope began to fade.

Galar let the thought ride the air.

Slowly, Gem was realizing who was responsible for the flood, and just how it had come about; how the many changes that developed over the past while had really impacted the group of four. And finally, the dire circumstances she was in sunk in...she was near blind and deaf without her extra mental faculties...and there would be no possibility of succor coming from Loni.

Tiny, unheeded tears slipped silently from beneath her half-closed eyelids.

There is really no choice here. My effectiveness is less than that of an average human being. I cannot get free...

"Do we have an agreement?"

"Yes."

I'll do anything to get free again. But when I am out of these chains...if I ever get my powers back again...you Galar...will be the first to pay!

"No funny stuff, now," he reminded her. "Or I'll hurt Flaw."

Not if I can stop you first...

"Okay," she agreed aloud.

I'll agree to anything, now. What happens in the future is still unknown; a different story.

"Well...I'm waiting for an answer."

"I said, okay! I agree."

But her words seemed to fall on deaf ears.

"Fine! Have it your way. You'll stay in here, without food or water, until it gets through that stubborn head of yours."

"But, I said, yes!" she declared emphatically.

He turned away. She rattled the chains; litterly screamed into his mind.

"I agree! I agree!"

He turned back.

"You got something to say?"

"Yes. I'll do whatever you want!"

But it appeared the man was as dull as the Neanderthal he resembled...or stone deaf.

"Well, I gave you your chance!"

He turned, pulled the light cord, relegating her to darkness. The door slammed. All the while Gemma screamed at him both mentally, and physically...until she was hoarse, and exhausted.

Still, he failed to understand.

The padlock was jammed home, and the tiny room filled with silence.

After a time, Gemma decided to see what she could still do. She tried to burn at the chains binding her. There was no small laser beam of red light shooting from her eyes, and no effect. Nor, when she touched the wall, could she will it to burn through...even a small hole. The accidental EM pulse frequency held her mind helplessly useless.

For three days, she languished. By the time Galar again opened the door, all Gemma wanted was water.

Yet, he would not give it to her, until she nodded vigorously, agreeing wholeheartedly to his plans.

There is no point in trying to communicate in any other way...

In her confinement, Gem had had much time to contemplate, and she had finally rationalized that Galar was deaf. It was the reason he did all the talking, and only because Scar was part of him, could he understand his own twin, and those talking to his brother.

Galar fed her dirty water, laced with blood, to drink, but...it was wet. What she gulped down, came back up again. He dragged her from her prison, left her chained, and lying in the gutter drain ditch, beneath where he was cutting up a dead woman. It was as if, he then forgot, she was there at all.

Chapter 24

Loni was boiling mad! He was so angry that, as he passed along the corridor the light bulbs along the way popped, and blew out. Until...the man calmed, and realized, he was exposing his power for all to see. Fortunately for him, no workers, or cameras, were near at hand.

For his own safety, Loni quickly willed the broken light fixtures to repair.

He had tried everything to find Gem. He finally deducted, that the only place left for Galar to hide her, was where he worked.

The first place he had searched was the twins' sleep quarters, but only Scar was there, asleep. He had entered his mind only briefly, just long enough to determined that the man knew nothing of the present whereabouts of the two. It angered Loni to realize the pair had worked together to corner her. He also knew, how brutally Galar had handled her.

Loni then search the showers, and lastly, the cafeteria, and had at last come to the conclusion, the only place left was Galar's work station. He had tried that door, only to be zapped.

He had expected something of that nature to happen. Then he travelled along the outside perimeter, looking for another way in. But everywhere Loni touched the walls, around the meat packing plant, he received an excruciating shock that sent him flying.

Loni was so angry, he would like to fry Galar's brain; if ever he got at him, he would do just that, even though he, and Gem, had made a pact never to use their powers to kill...

But what of in self-defense? Isn't this a case of protection, safeguarding one's mate? Gem was given to me! First!

He was determined to keep trying to get in; to find his girl.

Loni knew, it was pointless to ask the overseers for help. They would only laugh, because he had lost the female given into his care. They'd say it was his own fault; he had been lax.

Besides, Loni would have to use telepathy to tell them; they wouldn't understand any other way.

It wasn't worth the risk. He was on his own to get Gem back.

****

Da was upset. He didn't know what to do, and he couldn't find Loni to tell him what was happening.

He and Lydia had done okay alone, for the first while, but Loni had been gone a long time. As the older man had taught Da, the couple lived comfortably, up by the waterfall. Da would bring home the food, fruit from the stands, water from the drip pool at the side of the huge plunging waterfall.

Da took Lydia to work each day; protected her in the showers, cuddled her at night.

He never fed Lydia the meat dishes anymore, and she hadn't gotten sick for many a morning. She had shown him how her belly had swollen, told him the little round thing inside was his baby. They had created it together while playing.

The little thing kicked at Lydia sometimes, and when he touched her belly, Da too felt the movement against his hand. It sent shivers of excitement through him, and many an hour, the two spent laughing, and giggling over the phenomenon; petting their baby.

Lydia said, when it was big enough, it would come out.

He knew that!

Da had witnessed a birth many times, peeking from above in the rafters of the hospital.

His baby was still too small to come out, yet.

The ball that was a baby continued to grow, and still Loni stayed gone. Da didn't know why; neither he nor Gem ever came back.

Perhaps, they have been given a place of their own?

But they didn't come to work, either.

One day, Lydia appeared weaker than usual. She kept doubling over, holding her belly, as if it hurt her.

Baby is being naughty. I will let Lydia rest a bit.

Da kept digging the plot they were preparing. It was time for a different round of vegetables at this place in the garden.

Out of nowhere, the overseers came, snatching Lydia away with them. Da dropped his shovel, and made to follow, but they prevented him.

He waited. Went back to work; waited some more.

When Lydia had not returned by sleep time, Da went to the showers alone. He ate his meal, then slept by the waterfall, as usual.

The days passed slowly. Da did as he had every day; went to work, labored alone all day, showered, obediently eat only from the fruit stand, slept alone, and repeated the process again the next day...and the next; and the next.

He was very lonely; no one to share a companionable meal; no one to play with; no baby to pet...no Lydia. He went searching for Loni.

He will know what to do.

But no Loni...or Gem either. And there was no one else who understood him...who could read his thoughts so well...only Loni. And he had gone away too far to be found.

Da went back to the job.

Now, weeks later, as he watered the new plants in his fresh plot, two overseers brought Lydia back to him. He was so glad to see her, at first he didn't notice the changes. He didn't think to try to challenge the men, before they were gone again.

He hugged his returned mate with enthusiasm, near crushing her against him, but she was so limp and lethargic she just sat there. She flinched when he touched her face, his gesture questioning. She did not want to play.

He realized, then, she was hurt. Her clothing was covered in dry, and wet, red blood. Da took her to the showers, where he stripped her, and let the hot water run over her naked body.

She always liked that before.

That was when he realized, something was different.

As he used a cloth to bathe her, he noticed the little ball-belly was soft and near flat. He growled with anger, understanding quickly what had happened.

They have stolen our baby!

And that meant only one thing. It had been one of the dreaded girl babies.

But, I like girls! They aren't bad! I want my baby!

The thought of the tiny thing dying, brought tears coursing down his whiskered cheeks.

And they have hurt Lydia bad, too!

As he sponged her, the water kept running away crimson with blood. No matter how often he let the liquid run between her legs, the stream came away red.

He finally pulled her out of the shower fall, got a large clean towel, and tied it, diaper like around her hips. He got a new laundered dress, and clothed her, wrapped her in a blanket, and carried her up to the waterfall campsite.

Lydia listlessly lay on their mat, quietly sobbing, inconsolable.

Da resolved, he wasn't going back to work until Lydia was well again. The whole thing angered him, hurt him near as much as his mother-woman.

How could they do this? I will get our baby back! Just as soon...as Loni comes.

Trouble was, he didn't dare leave Lydia alone, to go look for him.

Loni will take care of Lydia, while I go recue the girl baby...

He knew they didn't kill the aborted infants right away. Some they kept in incubators; others even survived to grow bigger.

Da knew where they kept them, to study why they were different. And he had seen what some of the overseers did to girl babies...

They do bad things...they play grownup with them...

Da knew that was wrong!

I have to get the wee thing back. If only Loni would come home...fix Lydia, like he always fixes my hurts. Then...I can go recue belly-ball.

****

Lydia just wanted to die; she wanted this nightmare all to end. Mother would say, she was being punished, for being promiscuous.

She would be wrong! I've died, and gone to hell!

She had known right from the first, the minute the water started rising around the plane; there was no ever going back to her husband and first baby.

When Da offered comfort, she couldn't resist, and what followed was only natural.

She and Da had been so happy; he was like a small child treasuring the gift they had been given. He waited expectantly the arrival of this new born.

And with one stroke of their knife, the heartless physicians had ended all that. They hadn't asked her if that was what she wanted. The monitor had shown a girl, and apparently, that was a death sentence for this her second child.

Even on the table, she had bled profusely, almost as if her body was weeping after what it had lost. It wouldn't have been so bad if it had been a miscarriage, but to have them deliberately cut away her second baby...the loss was beyond endurance.

Her first husband and baby were lost to her forever, and now...a second little one, as well.

There was no reason to live. Let the blood ebb her life away. She didn't care...and would not fight!

Chapter 25

As the days passed, Gem near forgot there had ever been a brighter, pleasanter side to life. Loni's memory receded, and Galar became her focus; her only source of provision.

When finally, he took the chains off, she simply lay at his feet, resigned, too weak to fight, any mental abilities useless.

As Galar worked above her, Gem had very little view of her world, and not much awareness, of sound either. To her, the constant drone of the buzz saw was the essence of her new world.

She learned to feel an almost empathic sympathy for the crippled worker, as he struggled, hobbling about, on his crutch and one leg, dividing the various cuts of meat.

It was seldom he was given a human carcass; most were goat, pig, and sometimes a whole cow. These last, he had to kill himself...she later learned, this meat was for the elite, the Physicians who worked away, and returned on leave. They were used to better fare than human.

Galar would confine his livestock between iron stanchions, the head stationary, and when it finally stopped its struggle, he slammed it between the eyes with a gun-like ramrod. The animal immediately dropped, like a sack of limp grain; then the man quickly slit its throat, raising the carcass with a winch, catching the blood, of which he himself partook, before he passed it on to be used to make a blood sausage at another department.

He offered Gem this warm drink, but she refused to indulge.

After the creature was drained, came the skinning, and quartering, which went slow, with only one man, as Galar's twin remained absent. Gem soon realized why he needed a helper. It was messy, and unwieldly, especially for one so handicapped.

At last, Gem softened toward him, and out of pity, began to help him. At first, Galar was impatient, and down right rough with her, but despite this, with slight memory of any other treatment, Gem began to form an attitude toward him, that was little short of attachment.

The work became much easier, and Galar began to change, also. He constantly prattled on to himself, not expecting her to answer; as she had realized, so did he, that they couldn't talk to each other.

He explained, how he wasn't allowed to eat this privileged food, nor was he fortunate, like those who worked the gardens. He was restricted, only allowed human meat, no vegetables or fruit, except on special occasions, when he was permitted to go to the cafeteria. Sometimes, he supplemented his diet by catching rodents that ran through the gutters.

Galar began to cheat some, tossing Gem chunks of raw meat from the grinder, as he made sausage from human parts. Because these beings were received long after death, they were the old; tough, and some of the parts were already decaying, not good for much more than, what he called, hamburger. The very thought of eating it, turned Gemma's stomach.

She refused all such morsels, but finally, one night, hunger got the better of her, and Galar, feeling benevolent, built a fire of straw and sticks, in the center of a metal aisle, between the butchering stalls. Over this, he allowed her to roast her piece of meat.

Half heartedly, she eat, then, but...it wasn't long after, it all came back up again. From that he deduced, she couldn't stomach his usual food fare.

Galar brought her a wheat type porridge, then. Even that, came back several times, before she finally tolerated it. It seemed like months before Gem kept even a small amount of food down. Her belly swelled, but her body was thin and emaciated.

When she was finally strong enough to hold down the pieces of meat for the grinder, he rewarded her by stealing portions of pork or goat for her. Roasted, these sections were savory and juicy; nothing in memory had ever tasted so good, and best of all...it stayed down.

They never went to bathe. Galar did not trust her outside the slaughter house walls. Also, he was rather an uncleanly fellow, and preferred she be like him. He had no awareness that females might be different.

Water was scarce in the butchery, mostly used to wash away blood from the carcasses. Sometimes, when Galar's back was turned, Gemma snuck a drink beneath the running tap; washed her face and hands quickly, before he saw.

The man's preferred beverage of choice was cow's milk, taken from the udder before he knocked the beast into oblivion. That suited Gemma just fine...as long as it hadn't stood for days until it soured, and grew a green slime.

At night, Galar lay on a filthy mat, covered with spatters of blood from nearby kills, crawling with lice and bed bugs; the air above it thick with straw dust and dirt. Until the allergy she developed spent itself, Gemma sneezed continually when lying beside him.

Only once, did Galar try to be intimate with her. His hand pushed tentatively at the matted, tangled curls about her face with an almost tender motion, his intention obvious, as his other hand was exploring down her leg. Gemma drew away in abject fear, her eyes pools of terror, he couldn't mistake. As she moved across the pad, to the very opposite side, and settled in the straw beside it, in a crouch, as if about to flee, he accepted the inevitable, decided to forestall for another time, and let her go.

Ever after, she made her bed in the straw beside his pad, and did not sleep with him.

****

One day Scar finally returned. The two men were arguing loudly when Gemma awoke. She knew, she dare not interrupt, so she crouched on her knees to the side of them, waiting.

"You have forgotten me," accused Scar. "Have I no place now?"

"He's still looking for a way through," Galar scolded. "You need to stay away until he forgets her. Why did you come here? You've shown him the way in!"

"No, I haven't; he was on the far side. He's given up on this side..."

"Stupid! It doesn't matter. Why did you come? Can't you take care of yourself?"

"I was lonely," moaned the other. "I'm all alone. No one will be my friend. I miss you... Why have you cast me out?"

"I didn't! It's only until he forgets..."

"I have nothing to do...I watch all the others work, but I have no job..."

"Fine! Come back, then. Stay!" Galar gave in angrily. "We will share her."

Gemma cringed, and slunk away. Galar turned suddenly, grabbed her by the hair, and dragged her back. She knew, it was pointless to struggle.

After that, Galar was rough and impatient with her, again. But, the three soon learned to work as a unit. It was apparent, Scar was once more the preferred companion. Gemma was merely the side-line attraction.

She was given the duty of cooking the meat for them. Scar seemed to come and go freely. He often brought porridge back, and sometimes, stolen root vegetables, from which, Gem would make a soup.

Always, the two men kept her between them as they slept. Scar placed his mat on the other side of her straw strip. Neither man, ever, invited her onto his padded mattress. Which was fine with Gem; she hated the bugs that went with it.

****

Loni had given up. As he sat under a tree contemplating his failure, he suddenly remembered an incident from childhood:

When he had first been separated from his mother, at the age of twelve, work was unknown to him; his surroundings unfamiliar; Galar and Scar were appointed to teach him the ways of his new reality, to show him where things were, and what was required of him.

But, the pair considered him a burden, and so, much of the time, Loni was left on his own. He either tagged along behind the two older boys, or went exploring on his own, in his free time, always with the idea of finding, and reconnecting with his mother. It wasn't long, and Loni had learned well the lay of the entire Dome metropolis.

It consisted of two main systems: the inner core, which housed the cattle, and the butchery, where meat was cut, and meals prepared, for both the elite, and workers. The outer ring was all landscaped orchard, and gardens, including the gigantic waterfall, feeding the irrigation system. Out beyond the edges of this, were the guardian posts, observation screens, cafeteria, showers, and living quarters.

Above everything was a second floor; here were the exam rooms; operating and birthing areas, the Physicians' quarters, the nurseries and pregnancy holding rooms.

Hidden back of all that was a secret quarter where few were allowed: the science and experimental labs.

Here also, was the supercomputer that ran the establishment.

Traveling through every unit in the Dome's system were tunnels for sewer; with fat electric, and computer cables, strapped to the ceiling. Monstrous station rooms held gigantic boilers, and sent huge pipes, running both hot and cold water, through secondary tunnels.

As with all children, who tag along with their elders, Loni was considered a nuisance in the eyes of Galar. He sought, in any way possible, to rid himself of his pest.

One day, Loni found the entrance of a clean surface drainage tunnel. This led in from the world up top and outside, and the water was suppose to be filtered, and treated before it went into the overall system. Rumor had it that anything from out there was poisonous, contaminated, and deadly.

When it rained out there, the water came in freezing cold, pouring in dangerously swift, so an iron barred grate was used to close it off. But those maintaining it were lax, and only slid a bar across the outside, leaving the padlock hanging open. This way, they could easily access the tunnel to remove the debris that accumulated there.

Curious, Loni crawled into the tunnel, not realizing the grate should not have been left open, leaving the gate swinging. He also, was unaware Galar was following him.

When Loni returned after hours of exploration, he found Galar waiting on the other side of the padlocked grate. Chuckling with delight at his prank, Galar left his unfortunate victim crying, shouting after him to be released.

The next morning, after a freezing night jammed against the grate, while the water battered against his defenseless body, near drowned, the overseers found Loni, and set him free.

Thinking now of that uncomfortable time, Loni realized, that grate, and the drain tunnel could be the answer to his dilemma; his...and Gem's, ultimate salvation. From that upper system, led many a side tunnel, and one fed right out from the sewers of the butchery. And even better, this sewer drain was not controlled by the normal computer system, so maybe...Galar had not electrified it.

****

Enough with this!

Galar was through waiting.

Gem was submissive to his every whim; she never defied, anymore. She wasn't the problem.

It was Scar!

That big baby never leaves my side...never gives us long enough to be alone...to do anything.

He needed time to persuade this girl to fill his real needs. Galar wanted to be intimate with her, without Scar interfering or needing inclusion.

Besides, I need to seal the union, make her truly mine...if nothing else.

Scar is so stupid! He has no desires of his own, no arousal...he doesn't understand. He's like a small child...

In annoyance, Galar grabbed Gem's arm, turned angrily to Scar, and curtly ordered:

"You stay here! Don't follow us, you hear?"

Scar nodded, and returned to grinding the sausage meat, unperturbed.

Galar headed toward the sewer tunnel. He knew the perfect place to have privacy.

Chapter 26

Gem didn't even try to struggle, and after they had entered the reeking sewer passage, Galar allowed her to walk on her own; first beside him; then she followed behind.

Where is he going? What can he possibly want in here?

This sewer passage was different than the others. It did not have the electrical wires above, usually prevalent in most. It was darker, also noisier. Gem could hear rushing water in the distance.

She also felt different in here, more alert, and...she could see and hear better.

The blocking EM frequency does not extend this far!

For almost an hour, Galar led them down. They walked through fetid, stagnant puddles that splashed at their bare ankles, and up the legs of their coveralls. Many times, Galar's crutch slipped on the green slime that covered the floor, lined the walls, and dripped from the roof of the large man-height, round tunnel.

It took all his effort for the man to proceed on his own, let alone, help the woman with him. Gem could easily have run away, but where was there to go? Now, she was curious as to the purpose of the trip, so followed after, docilely.

Wonder where this leads? And...why is he so doggedly determined to take me there? What is at the other end?

After a long valiant struggle down the sloped passage, they finally reached a granite ledge. Here, as was Galar's habit, he began to warn himself.

"Watch out now, we don't want to go over the edge. It drops down hundreds more feet to the pit of Hades, where the Hydra lives. We feed him the remains of the dead, so he won't come up, and eat the rest of us, see?"

Gemma scoffed, nearly laughing.

Hydra! Bet that's just a silly story, told to frighten the men from going down here.

A long time ago, in what seemed like a lifetime past, she had done research on the Greek legend. The Hydra was a many headed, snake-like dragon, purposed to guard the gates of Hell.

Surely, there is no such thing...

If there was...

Now, wouldn't that just fit right into the conditions that exist in this place?

They moved on, sideways to the right, along the precarious shelf, for many yards; then, came to a metal ladder leading upward. Beginning the climb, Galar slung his crutch by a loop, around his neck, and over his back. Gem found the going easier than he.

The rungs of the ladder were dry, and the rust came away in a red powder on your hands. But, moisture hung in the air; the fresh smell of water up above...light, dim at first, yet gradually increasing in brightness.

With each step, Gemma felt stronger, was aware of more, heard better. Her mind was expanding, opening up. It felt good.

Could it be, her powers were awakening; returning? At last!

****

About an hour behind them, Loni had reached the junction leading into the sewer going up into the slaughter house. The over powering stench that emanated from the hole drew him up short.

He shuddered, not wishing to enter that horrible nightmare of a place. He had never actually gone in before, but he'd seen from other vantage points, what went on in there.

Loni had not even previously gone this far into the drainage tunnel.

The ledge upon which he stood was dangerously slippery, but he only had inches to go to enter the culvert that led up to where he needed to go, the cattle pens.

In there is the love of my life. I'll not be a coward. I will go through whatever it takes to get her back!

Yet, as he stood there, something else made him hesitate. His senses were recording not just the gagging vapors of the sewer beneath him.

Galar has been here...and not too recently, either...about an hour ago...going along this ridge...

And...there was a subtle scent just underneath his...the fragrance of a woman.

Gem! My Gem!

She is with him!

Abruptly, Loni changed direction, going down instead of up.

****

In the sausage plant, Scar had finished his work. All the while he had labored alone, he had mulled sullenly over the situation.

156

Scar had come to the conclusion, Galar meant to remove the female from his reach, to keep her for himself, alone. They were abandoning him, and that made Scar angry.

Galar said we would share her!

The more the man dwelt on the circumstances, the more wrathful it made him, until at last, Scar threw down his tool, and stomped after his brother into the sewer.

Once in the tunnel, he knew only the path to the ledge, and lacking the olfactory senses of one such as Loni, or the stored knowledge of the planners, he was decidedly disadvantaged. Instead of going in the right direction, he turned the opposite way, and though he searched many a side tunnel for the next few hours, he soon found himself desperately confused, and hopelessly lost.

*****

Galar and Gem climbed higher and higher. As they rose top ward, each foot, yard, and mile, brought from above, the most pleasant life-giving atmosphere imaginable. The feeling of well being increased, and Gem grew stronger, more alert, with a broader vision, and understanding.

Is this the way out that I've longed to find for so long? Is the surface above us? Can I finally escape, and go home?

Hope made her two hearts pound in anticipation, but when they finally stepped out on the second ledge, Gem dropped to her knees in both awe, and consternation.

Beyond, in the distance, stretched a landscape so vast, the valley went on for miles. But, it was definitely not the surface she had anticipated. Above them, the sky held a double moon, and the stars spread out like the rings of Saturn; the constellations unrecognizable.

The trees below, and beyond the stone shelf, were so thick they seem to touch, making a pathway off across, and over this world. Like a canopy of up-side-down umbrellas, inverted by the wind, made useless for keeping off the rain, the branches were like roots reaching upward, the leaves on them of a pink-gold shade. The trunks were a dark brown.

Unquestionably, not the trees of Earth!

Across to the nearest tree, someone had built an iron-girder, slat-type bridge with a wooden plank floor, and in the tree across, a small metal and canvas, dome-shaped, housing unit. Suddenly, seeing this, Gemma realized Galar's intent.

Not only was she trapped on another world, never to see her home again, but he planned to take her out alone, into the building yonder, and ravish her in private, uninterrupted.

It was too much!

Never!

In rebellion, Gemma lay down flat upon the stone ledge, refusing to be dragged an inch farther.

She wouldn't let this filthy being touch her like that!

When Galar reached down to pull her up, Gem had gathered just enough psychic energy to raise her shield. The resulting force, zapped him so hard, it sent him flying, and the woman went down mentally, into a physical faint, from the effort.

Chapter 27

Gem came to reality, trembling, and unbearably weak; it had taken all her reserve to send that warning voltage.

Distantly, a faint, desperate voice called out for help, in panic.

Vaguely, in a fog of mental confusion, Gem surveyed her surroundings, wondering where she was.

Rock on two sides; the sweet smell and sound of fresh rain, and beneath that the unpleasant odor of a reeking, unwashed body; her own. Her face was wet from the raindrops; the gravelly clay beneath her, made slippery by puddles formed in a downpour.

She lay there confused.

The urgent voice turned to a scream, calling to her to give it aid. It was not simply a tone of sound, but a mental anguish she could sense and feel, shouting loud and clearly in her head.

Galar? Where is he?

She rolled to her side, toward the distressed sounds; her vision cleared, showing her the drop down ledge nearby, and beyond that, the scenic landscape. Now, Gemma recalled her previous clarification, what it meant to her situation, and what had happened just prior to her passing out.

Again, she heard Galar's desperate pleas for help. They were coming from beneath the edge of the nearby stone cliff.

Her vision seemed to split, as if she were in two heads at once. In the one, she clearly saw, with her own eyes, the stone edge, and one set of fingers, clawing to raise a suspended body.

From the mind of the other, she looked back and down, down, down; to the pit below, so deep the bottom could not be seen. Galar had lost his crutch, and his other arm waved toward the abyss, as if he were seeking to recapture what he had lost.

The shadows beneath him moved, wavy and unrecognizable.

Something is down there!

She felt the terrified panic of the man. He thought, the Hydra was beneath, rising to get him.

But, this isn't the same ledge. It can't be the Hydra.

Besides, it was just a story. Unless the abyss connected to the sewer drop, no predator could slip into this valley.

Could it?

Anyway...the Hydra isn't real.

Yet this was not her human world...anything was possible.

His fear spread to her, and drove her to instant action. No matter what he was, or what he had done, he didn't deserve to die like this!

Gem crawled forward, her hand extended. Grabbing the groping fingers, she gave them a leverage. He clutched at the offered assistance, as a man desperate for his last breath of air, his grip like a steel vise...and nearly pulled her over with him.

She had no support. Fearful for her own safety, she eased back, leaving him clawing at the air, but fortunate for him, he got purchase with his second hand.

I need something to use to tie myself to...

Vines climbed along the outer stone, near the edge. With one of these, she tied her legs, then, with a second trailing end, she went forward again, allowing one of his seeking fists to get purchase on the rope-like branch. With her other hand, she reached out to clasp the hand against the ledge.

Slowly, inch by inch, his head, then his shoulders, came above the cliff. He was almost over, and then...

Behind him rose the most gruesome apparition: a horned, snake-like head of purple and green, eyes glowing red, jaws open, and dripping saliva. A second beside the first, and a third waving behind the others.

Gemma screamed; at the same time, so did Galar. But he was the nearer, and the first monster jaws...took his head.

Whether she reasoned out what she did, cannot be determined; that Galar was already dead with the first bite, would have been evident.

Gemma let go, at the same time as reflex released Galar's fist from the vine. His body flew back with the force of the two-fold liberation, tumbling into the abyss behind. The Hydra heads dived after it, anxious for the whole meal...forgetful of the second tasty morsel on the ledge.

Gemma slunk away to the farther most corner, behind a large rock, hugging herself, the faintest mewling sound escaping her, like a lost kitten fearful and lost.

And then, Loni was there; enfolding her in his arms; holding her, comforting her. Yet, Gemma believed it was part of her dream; a nightmare to torment her. Madness came close, haunting her, and finally, she escaped into oblivion.

Chapter 28

Loni was almost at the top of the ladder, when he heard the dreadful screams. It sounded like both Gemma and Galar were screaming at each other. When he popped his head above the hole into open air, all was ominously silent, except for a plaintive moaning from something hidden behind a huge rock in a far corner.

As Loni crawled out into the open, his eyes opened wide in disbelief, spying the rocky ledge, and the vision of the world beyond it; a place he had heard of only in his mother's stories: two moons on the horizon, the stars of the night sky in the shape of gigantic rings; trees with up-side-down roots, reaching upward, as if in supplication to a god that had forgotten them, and even in the distance, reptiles...not seen since prehistoric times; that should have been long extinct.

Those that had gone into the domes for shelter, a long time ago, had declared the surface unlivable, the atmosphere poisonous, but as Loni tested the air, he detected nothing deadly. All he smelled was the sweet scent of fresh rain; saw only the misting of moisture covering all within sight with a wet film.

He stepped out on to the slippery surface, fully expecting attack; awaiting Galar to speedily fall upon him, but all that his senses found, was the faint whimpering from behind the far sheltering rock in the corner.

Where is Galar? What did he do with Gem?

Cautiously, Loni approached the shelter, from behind which came the pitiful sound. Even before he saw her, his nose was assaulted by the most horrendous stench, evidencing her presence.

Who...what is this ugly creature? This cannot be...Gem!

She reeked like the sewer; her hair matted, and litterly moving with vermin. Lice!

The coveralls she wore were stiff with dried blood, fecal matter, and small scraps from animal kills. Her feet were bare, but unrecognizable as those belonging to a female, so covered in sewer slime, and caked dirt, were they.

She had curled away toward the wall, in a fetal position, her dirty, scratched, bare arms, wrapped across her almost non-existent chest; her raised knees covering, and near hiding, the swollen abdomen. But, Loni saw, anyway.

Oh, man! She is pregnant!

Loni shivered, fearing the worst. Galar had taken advantage.

He knew, this hapless woman could only be his Gem. Her skin coloring was not the tanned brown of the other race; it was white-blue like his own; the result of the introduction of his DNA match. If he doubted, even the slightest, there was her eyes, and even though, at this moment, they stared dark, and vacant, the whites shone in the half-light, as did his, and the centers were that beautiful turquoise blue...like his mother's.

When Loni crouched down beside her, Gem flinched in fear. Despite what that implied, Loni felt relief. It gave him confidence, she had not let Galar have his way with her...at least not easily.

She tried to crawl away, but there was nowhere to go. Cringing at the touch of her, the man pulled his loved one against him, determined to minister to her no matter how offensive her physical condition was. Loni gathered Gem close, holding her tightly, until the trembling lessened.

He quickly realized, there had never been any intimacy with Galar.

How long has it been since she has been touched in a gentle way? Even a baby dies for lack of fond caress; a woman shrivels with such neglect.

And indeed, Gem had shriveled...to nothingness...both physically and mentally.

Loni's hand slid over her belly, caressing, easing...but mostly, to see if the baby still lived. It did not move.

Barely alive. And...the child is too far along even to be Galar's. He is not the father. This child is mine!

Loni invaded Gem's mind, searching for what had transpired in the interval she had been lost to him. And came away shocked, both by the fact that her psychic abilities had been kept deficient, and were almost nil, even now; and at the appalling dealings at the hands of Galar and Scar...but most of all, at the horrific happenings of the past few hours.

Loni was almost relieved at the death of Galar...almost, but not quite, joyous at the freedom so hideously gained. Even he agreed, he wouldn't wish such a death on his worst enemy.

Yes, at times, I wanted to kill the man, but it was merely anger speaking. Never...like this!

Loni shivered at the memory he'd read.

Will she ever, again, be the same happy Gem I once knew?

****

Once she had passed into a fitful dream sleep, limp and unconscious, Loni raised his unresisting burden, and slung her across one shoulder. He started down the ladder, on the long journey home. He had little choice, but to return to the inner dome. Loni knew nothing of the valley below the ledge, of the surface, and inside, all was familiar. There, he could help Gem, tend to her needs, maybe even, heal her psyche.

He would not take her through the slaughter house, but he would have to pass by there, to get through to the rainwater drain grate.

****

Scar was so lost, he had sat down, and given up, yet if he had only realized it; he was right next to the main drain tunnel. In his mind, it was okay if he died in here.

It is better than being alone.

He felt as if he, and Galar, had been torn apart, forever; more so than at any other time. He had sensed the rip a short while before; like suddenly Galar was no longer there...had ceased to exist.

Scar didn't know the meaning of dead, but that is what he remotely reasoned had taken place.

Maybe, Flaw killed Galar; that's why I can't feel him..

Just as he was thinking of the blue-skinned man, Scar heard a grunt, and felt the wall next to him vibrate, as if someone carrying a heavy burden had slipped, and hit the rock behind.

Scar lifted his head, abruptly alert. His thoughts went immediately to his own needs.

Maybe, whoever it is, can lead me out of here?

He peered around the corner cautiously; the man was moving slowly away, a body slung over his back.

That's Flaw!

At first, Scar thought the body the man carried was his brother, but he quickly realized it was that of a woman.

He has our female...or...does it belong to Flaw, again?

No matter. Maybe it is better not to have her. Galar and I can be together again, this way.

He drew back, once more, until the man was near out of sight. Then, Scar followed after, at a safe distance.

****

The first place that Loni went, was to the showers.

When he had touched her stomach, Loni had realized much more about Gem than her simple pregnancy. She had gone through periods of violent vomiting, sever lack of appetite, and at times, bouts of ravenous hunger. At some point, Galar had force fed her raw, or half-cooked rancid meat. Because of this, her belly was infested with worms, which constantly competed for the nourishment both she, and the small one needed. That was why Gem was nothing but skin and bones.

Loni knew how to purge her; he'd watched the physicians do it many times. And this was the perfect time. While she was unconscious, she wouldn't feel a thing.

Or so he thought...

As he set the mask over her face, and watched while the machine pumped out the contents of her stomach, Loni couldn't help but marvel, how the physicians never seemed affected by the patient's discomfort.

He sensed every upheaval, and elimination, and was feeling quite ill by the time the lower bowel also had been

167

emptied. And the treatment to prevent further infestation, was no better. Near the end, Loni was gagging in reflex.

It seemed impossible, even though Gemma was listless, and barely aware, that she did not feel his cruel ministrations. Yet, he knew, it was all necessary, for her future well being...and that of the infant she carried. Neither would survive, if this were not done.

The inner finally dealt with, Loni took Gem again into the shower section, to restore the exterior. First thing he did was attack the hair. All her once beautiful silver-blond curls were so matted, and infested with lice, he felt crawly just touching it. There was no way he could untangle it, or rid her of the moving pests, except to shave her.

It will grow back again...just a matter of time. My poor, poor Gem.

He wouldn't touch the mass, simply allowed it to sluice away into the drain. Then he treated the scalp sores; disinfected against the eggs left behind.

He bathed her, every inch of her bruised, scraped, emaciated body, tenderly, carefully, halting purposely over the undersized swell of the baby bump, to treasure and caress. It brought tears to his eyes, but he swallowed back the emotion, and continued on.

At last, Loni clothed her in a fresh coverall, then wrapped his bride in a soft blanket.

Toward the end of his ministrations, Loni became aware of being watched. Back in the steam, by the far wall, crouched Scar. He had followed, like a predator, observing, waiting, as if to take back what he thought belonged to him.

She isn't yours, Scar. I will not let you hurt her again.

Watch carefully. Maybe, you will learn how to tend a female; to treat her with dignity and affection?

Loni carefully hoisted his unconscious loved one into his arms, and stood. He made for the waterfall campsite.

Let him follow, but...I will fight you for her, if I have to.

Yet Scar did not follow. The next time the two men were to meet, Scar would be clean, and wearing fresh garments. If he had learned anything from observation, he applied it first to himself.

Chapter 29

Da lay beside Lydia, mourning. He was certain, if his girl was not already dead, she soon would be. Long ago, he had given up hope that Loni and Gem would come back to the waterfall nest.

Movement at the ladder, rising from below, made him lift his head. And there, at long last, came Loni, carrying Gem in his arms.

She was hurt, Da reasoned. They had done something to her, as they had to Lydia. It made him angry. But he quietly lay back to watch.

Loni is busy.

His mentor knelt down on his abandoned mat with his burden, unfurled Gem from the mantle that surrounded her, lay her out flat, and gently covered her with the blanket, again, tucking the edges tenderly about her like a cocoon. Then wearily, Loni lay down behind her.

It was then Da noticed, how very thin Gem had grown; and she was bald, as if someone had just recently shaved her. He also observed the small, swollen, abdomen, and his heart began to race with anticipation.

At least they didn't get the baby bump. Loni is going to be a poppa!

But Loni seemed less excited by the fact; he appeared rather depressed; thoroughly exhausted, almost sick, himself. It was only seconds, and he too was asleep.

Need to protect them.

But good intentions are often not easily kept. Da promptly fell fast asleep.

Da woke with a start. Loni and Gem were fighting; the sparks litterly flying.

At some point, Loni must have slipped away for food. He was attempting to feed Gem from a dish of porridge. At his first effort, she had sprung up rapidly from the pallet, batting at the spoon, sending it flying, backing toward the wall, not only giving off red and blue, wavy, static sparks, but hissing like a cornered cat. Startled from sleep, there was no telling what she envisioned; it was, as if she thought the dish held poison.

It was obvious, she either thought Loni someone else, or she no longer trusted him.

Da took advantage of the situation; as soon as Loni set the bowl aside, he fetched it for Lydia, crawling covertly after the spoon, and retrieving it, as well. Da found his mate, her eyes open, but filled with listless disinterest.

Unlike Gem, Lydia did not fight being fed. A spoonful at a time, went down, but he was able to coax her to swallow only two or three, before Lydia closed her eyes again in exhaustion.

Loni, on the other hand, had changed his tactics; he had offered Gem a small, ripe plum. Da watched, as for a second, Gem stared at the fruit in Loni's hand, as if she was having difficulty seeing it, then she grabbed for it, missed, and almost batted it from Loni's hand.

Patiently, carefully, Loni took her fist in his empty hand, opened it, and placed the tempting morsel in her palm. Hungrily, almost instantly, she was eating, greedily, juice dripping down her cheeks and chin.

What is wrong with her? It's like...she can't see!

Gem ate like a creature starving. Loni had to hold her back at times, or she would eat too quickly, or too much. At last, satisfied she'd had sufficient, Loni made her lay down again; sleep overcame her almost instantly.

With the women fed and asleep, the men filled their empty bellies, as well, and once more returned to slumber, also. Da was a simple fellow; now that Loni had returned, he expected that life would go on as usual.

And so the days followed, one after another, until Gem grew stronger.

But...Lydia did not.

****

Loni felt a tugging at his shirt. He had just brought back the gatherings of another meal, but Gem was still dozing. He turned about, to gazing into the pleading eyes of Da. The younger man's anguish was almost palpable. Da wanted him to follow him over to his mat.

Gem is resting still. Guess I can safely go see what is bothering him.

As Loni neared Lydia, he was bombarded, near overwhelmed, by the suffering he read in her mind, not to mention her physical condition.

How has this happened? When did this happen? How could I be so unaware?

Anger shot through Loni as he realized what had been perpetrated against the younger couple in his absence. Abruptly, guilt replaced that hot feeling, when he admitted, he might have prevented some of it, had he been there.

"You fix?" queried Da, pleadingly, by thought.

Loni stooped, knelt beside the despondent woman; skimmed his hand across the bloody towel covering Lydia's

private area. He had been so in attentive to the other couple; driven by his own needs and worries; only vaguely wondering, what Da was doing with the many towels. Da's back had always been toward them, as the younger man was cleaning his mate.

She's been bleeding a long time...and no longer has the will to live...near death. What can I tell him?

Loni sighed.

"I can't fix her, Da," he thought projected. "A male of my kind can only heal his own mate...only help another female, and...Lydia is beyond...my help."

As the impact of what Loni had revealed hit home to Da, he began to moan in anguish, groaning as if it were he with the death sentence. He began carrying on so loudly, sobbing unrestrained, brokenly, inconsolable; Loni felt the very depth of his grief.

When Loni tried to comfort, Da drew away almost angrily, pushing his arms away, rejecting the offered comfort. There was no consoling him.

****

Gradually, Gem's abilities had been returning. She could now see her surroundings quite clearly, hear the sounds around her, the waterfall, the birds in the trees. She could even, once again, read Loni's thoughts. At last, she was beginning to feel comfortable around him again, safe.

But, what was that god awful racket that had awakened her?

Sleepily, she had been remotely aware, when Loni had moved away with Da; she had lazily, slowly, eased back from slumber to reality. With full wakefulness came clarity.

That's Da! Why is he so upset?

Gem sat up. Vaguely, she could make them out across the trampled dirt of the camp, under the spreading spruce tree, standing there, near Da and Lydia's bed. Still unsteady, she got to her feet; over balanced by the weight of her baby, she nearly went down again, but managed to right herself quickly. She moved quietly over to the pair, unnoticed.

Before she got to the struggling men, Gem noticed Lydia. For a moment, the woman's condition brought her to a shocked standstill beside her friend.

From the simple, unshielded mind of Da, Gem instantly read all that had happened. He had never been able to cloak his thoughts, or his memories, against her probes.

And Loni also was easy, being so preoccupied with quieting Da, and not realizing the necessity to close his mind to her. Gem immediately found, and knew, what needed to be done.

Before Loni was even aware of her presence, Gem had knelt beside the dying girl, taken Lydia's hand, and traded damaged female organs, for better health and vitality. The Healer only stopped short at replacing her own baby for that which had been lost...

As Gem slumped to the ground beside the pad, Loni turned, finally noticing her.

Chapter 30

Loni let out a howl of despair, when he realized what Gem had done. All he had accomplished in his days of gentle care had now been undone...almost.

He knew, now, she really needed a physician's intimate care, but...he couldn't bring himself to subject her to that. He dare not take her to them; he knew what they would do to her. She would never be safe in their hands.

The races under the domes had always had things backward. The real Healing gene was in the white skinned race; the dark males envied the ability, and tried desperately to usurp it. Instead of venerating the competent female talent, they did their best to eliminate the genuine Healers. It had never been because they were female; not about man verses woman; only the white skin, supposedly inferior, and the brown skin superiority, but no matter how hard they tried, all they had done was demonize the craft with their horrific experiments, and imitations.

The dark ones had the dense gene.

No, Loni couldn't take Gem to them!

He knelt, grieving that she had healed too soon, yet knowing, the life of the other was important, also. He lifted Gem to his arms, and quietly moved back to his own pad.

So, once again, Loni began his gentle ministrations. She was hemorrhaging; bad for the baby. It must be stopped quickly.

He sent Da for more towels. Life took on the constant ritual of the sickroom.

****

Lydia was not her cheerful self. The loss of her second child weighed heavily still, even though Gem had healed her body. If they let her, Lydia would stare off into space the whole day long. So every chance he got, Loni used her and Da to fetch and carry. Sometimes, he sent the two together, or most often, he split them up, leaving Da to guard Gem, and taking Lydia with him.

Today was such a time. Loni and Lydia were getting the day's rations.

Loni had just loaded Lydia, and was about to send her ahead. They had developed a system, using the backpacks, and all four plates, and cups, so they could take more at a time, and would not have to return every meal.

He hadn't yet sent her on her way; Loni was grabbing the last fruits, stuffing his pack full, when he was seized rudely from behind, and spun around to face the burly guard.

"What you think you are doing, Flaw?" the man yelled in Loni's face.

Instead of showing attention immediately, Loni quickly, mentally projected an order to Lydia: "Run! Get out of here, before he notices you."

And for once, whether from past memory of abuse, or what, Lydia came out of her lethargic inattention, and obeyed promptly. She quickly slipped among the trees, and was gone.

At least the others will get fed.

Loni played the mute, humbly standing by submissively, as the enforcer pawed through what he had in his backpack. It wasn't much, only fruit; Lydia had the rest.

"Fruit?" the man muttered disdainfully. Then, after thinking on it for a minute, he challenged. "Where is your mate, Flaw? You get her back? Is she hidden, so you can keep her?"

The man laughed, making certain Loni saw his face, and his lips move.

Loni nodded vigorously.

"Where you staying, now?" the guard asked. "I checked your lodgings. It's been wrecked by water; you haven't been there in months. Can't say I blame you," he added. "For not staying in there. It smells of mildew, and the walls are growing mold, but...where the heck ARE you living?"

Loni raised both hands above his head, in a gesture meant to signify lack of knowledge, shrugged his shoulders for emphases, and pointed around at the trees.

The guard laughed. "You living free and easy, camping under the trees, like a nomad? Well, I'll be. How convenient. But, you listen here. You're lucky I'm alone right now...another guard wouldn't be this easy on you. You can't just take food without doing your share...yeah, I noticed you haven't been to work in some time. I'll let you go today, but you can't goof off any more. You better all be at work tomorrow, you understand? Make sure you bring No Name, too. You hear?"

Loni nodded energetically.

His pack was handed back to him; yet Loni still waited until the overseer had turned his back, and strode away. When he was out of sight, Loni quickly blended into the surrounding trees, where there were no cameras, so he would not be seen, or followed.

****

His worst fears had been realized; the dreaded day had come.

Loni and Da had helped their two women to the work site, but they had little energy to be of any use. Lydia could dig, and lug things; she and Da worked well together, but the woman had little desire for life, and simply sat there, if you didn't prod her.

Gem sat down to weed; her level of energy depleting quickly.

Their work patch had become so over grown, the weeds were taller than the infant seedlings. At least, before all had been abandoned, Da had done a replanting.

Between them, they had managed two days of constant maintenance, bringing the patch to near normal, again. Then the overseers came around to check on them; and...they also noticed Gem's condition. Of course, they had to report it.

A short time later, using their usual method of communication, Loni was accosted, rudely grabbed from behind, and spun around to face the messenger.

"Flaw! Listen! Bring your females to the Physicians. They haven't had a check up in a while. You understand?"

Loni nodded.

What else could he do? If he didn't comply, they would forcefully take the women, whether he liked it or not.

Now, quaking with dread of what might happen, Loni stood with the other three, waiting in line to be seen.

****

With Da on the other side of the examining table on which she sat, a Physician stood over Lydia. He had just finished the full body scan. Uncomfortable and rebellious, Lydia sat up as soon as he was finished.

Da didn't need to be told how much she hated the Physicians now. Gem and Loni could also sense the anger in both of them.

Lydia's doctor turned to the Physician still examining Gem; spoke with satisfaction in his voice, as he addressed his companion.

"This one has recovered quite nicely. Think we should separate the pair...try another male?"

The other shook his head. "Naw. They mate well. Give No Name another chance to father a male. The last one they had may have been female, but it's still healthy."

The first nodded in agreement.

"How is Flaw's partner?"

The second man, stepped away from Gem, huffing in disgust. "I can't figure how she got this bad off...needs a better diet, and more rest. She is so close to term...it's a little late now. And, this stupid monitor won't show me the sex...faulty again!"

Both Loni and Gem knew what was wrong with the instrument, but neither would ever tell. Gem had willed the screen to go fuzzy. Loni heaved a sigh of relief when she was successful.

He knew his offspring was a female, also, and if they ever found out, they'd do to Gem what they had done to Lydia...only they would kill his child. It would come out white.

From the conversation between the two Physicians, Loni realized, they were still keeping Da and Lydia's baby alive; experimenting... Something needed to be done about that!

"Should we keep the pregnant one here, maybe?"

Loni cringed.

"Naw. No need for that. I think she's better off active. Send her back with Flaw...see that she's given a protein supplement."

Over my dead body! They use human meat to make that!

Loni resolved to throw those away, as soon as they were given the capsules.

****

With relief, Loni lead the way out of the med center, but at the door, was abruptly brought up short by a large door guardian. He was gripped by the shoulders, and pulled up close to the face of the bearded giant.

"Hold up, Flaw! The Review overseer wants a word with you. He needs a few questions answered. Bring the other three along."

The four followed obediently, to stand before a desk in another room. As they waited for the director to look up, and deal with their case, Loni gazed about apprehensively.

What was it all about?

It was then, Loni noticed Scar, standing off to the side. His two hearts began knocking together in panic; fear became the taste in his mouth.

The Director stood up, rounded the desk, so he was next to Loni. He was irate; meant to get right up and personal. When Loni backed away, the hulking beast seized him by the shoulders. Stooping a bit, the Director made certain they were eye to eye. He shouted to make sure Loni would not mistake his attitude.

"Do you understand me, Flaw?"

Shivering, Loni nodded.

"Good! Now...WHERE...IS...GALAR?"

Loni swallowed with difficulty; chose to pretend innocence. Shrugged.

"Did you kill him?"

That one Loni could answer honestly.

Loni's eyes went wide, an excellent imitation of shocked innocence.

"Don't you con me!" growled the Director.

Suddenly, threateningly, a huge guard, twice her size, forced Gem up next to them. At his first touch, she let out a startled, terrified squeak, and stood trembling.

The Director turned to address her.

"Did your she kill him?"

The large guard shook Gem violently for emphasis. Loni watched as her eyes filled with uncertainty, then guilt, and finally confusion.

The Director turned back to Loni.

"Did she?"

There was no pretending he didn't understand. No time for that. Loni shook his head, emphatically, terrified at what they might do to Gem.

It was a fact, neither he nor his mate had done away with Galar, but Loni knew, Gem felt responsible. She had shocked Galar, sending him over the ledge. And even though she had tried to save him, Gem had released Galar at the end.

The guard peered closely into Gem's terrified eyes. She was trembling visibly. Loni felt her irrational fright of the colossal male; a dread he meant her to feel, yet there was nothing Loni could do to comfort, or reassure.

"I don't think they know anything about it," declared the man that held Gem.

The Director nodded. "Scar is either mistaken, or..."

At a movement of the director's head, the guard abruptly let Gem go. Both men turned to look toward Scar, who cringed, and seemed almost to shrink into himself under their scrutiny.

"Scar's probably the one guilty. He and his brother were no doubt fighting. Scar maybe got the upper hand, and now, he feels remorse. Had to blame someone, and Flaw was handy."

"Galar may simply have fallen down some drain hole, and couldn't get out. They are always fooling around by the ditches. Fact remains, Scar is alone...until Galar turns up, he needs supervision..."

The Director turned again to Loni.

"You!" he said. "You are good at handling misfits. Scar will join your group. He'll be issued new bedding, and necessities. He seems to have lost those he had. Take him with you!"

And with that, they were all dismissed.

Chapter 31

When he had Scar situated on a mat of his own, under a tree far enough away, he would not be a problem, Loni took time to sit down, and evaluate the situation.

There were two pressing emergencies looming: One, the women.

They were no longer safe by the waterfall. It was only a matter of time before those over them found where they spent their free time, and nights.

Loni needed to get Gem away from the Physicians, before the baby put in an appearance. They would definitely remove the child, after it was born. His own mother had hid him, but that likely wouldn't work a second time.

Now that Loni knew a way out, he had a place to go. However...it would take time to prepare for the escape, and he had too little time.

Secondly: Now that he was with them, how far could Scar be trusted? If Loni showed him the escape route, would Scar tell the overseers?

****

Scar didn't know how to act, so he stayed silent, watching. He knew Flaw from previously, and...the woman, but not her name. Galar had never called her by name.

Scar knew the other pair only as Flaw's work mates.

The four never spoke aloud, or rarely, anyway. Scar missed Galar's constant chatter.

It was days before he picked up their real names, and that only happened by accident, when one of the women caught the hand of a man to get his attention, and called him by name.

The dark, younger man was Da, not No Name, as the guards called him. Nor was Flaw known by the derisive moniker the overseers had given him. He was called Loni. Neither of these men ever spoke; Da made noises, and used gestures, but Loni seemed to have a way of communicating direct to the minds of the others.

The women called to each other, and that was how Scar learned their names, Lydia was the younger, despondent one; Gem or Gemma was the pregnant, frail one Galar had captured. She too, seemed able to make the others understand without any spoken word.

Loni and the two women were white skinned; actually Gem and Loni were more blue tint than anything, and Da was brown skinned, and dark haired, like Scar, himself.

Scar had been taught from birth, anyone of the light race was inferior, but he couldn't help but see...these blue people, Loni and Gem, were smarter even than Galar had been. And so, Scar chose to watch...and learned from them.

Loni was the undisputed leader, but unlike Galar, he led with a gentle hand. And apparently, he didn't demand total obedience; you could choose to do what you wished. Not like Galar: obey or else. Loni never punished...as far as Scar could tell.

Yet, the others most always did his bidding without questioning. They came and went by some silent orders, and...always returned. Da and Lydia brought food; more blankets, even pots from the storage area. It seemed, the four had the access key to supply.

After leaving the court room, where Scar had been thrown in with them; where it appeared only the accuser, Scar, had been given punishment, the group did not return to their work station, as Scar had expected. They detoured, first to the showers.

Scar felt he was clean; he'd not been working. The overseers had detained him in the court area all day.

In the shower, the other two men blocked Scar's view, until the women were dressed again, then first Da, and when he was finished, Loni, showered alone, while the other remained with the women.

When Loni went back into the steaming area, he dragged Scar with him. The new man had no choice, but to join in, and disrobe. It was like Scar had been compelled.

With their toilet finally finished, they went to the supply depot. After he had picked out his new property, Loni carried the new mat for Scar. This shocked him. Galar would never assist his twin with anything, even though he was the one with the two hands.

As they topped the ladder, Scar found they were at the top of the great waterfall, and was shocked a second time. A neat camp was spread out beneath the trees; each couple had their own bedding space apart from the other, and in the very center, was a communal feeding area with a small tri-pod over a circle of rocks. It was obvious, this was used to heat or cook, but at the moment, the wood was dry and unlit.

While Loni prepared a space for Scar, away from either of the others, the dark man, Da, and his mate, Lydia, disappeared down the ladder again. They took their back packs, and the plates and cups of the other couple, as well as their own. By the time they returned with food and beverages, Loni had Scar comfortable, and was sitting beside a sleeping Gem, obviously deep in thought.

Da and Lydia brought a considerable amount of food: plenty of fruit, breads, fruit juices, milk...but no meat. Scar missed meat, but...he loved fruit, so for now, it didn't much matter. He rushed forward, as was the usual practice, if he ate with Galar, to steal what he could, while he had the chance. However, he immediately rammed up against an invisible barrier, enclosing the area, where the spread was laid out on a cloth blanket.

That also, was the first time, he heard Loni in his head.

"Bring your plate and cup. And, you needn't fight...there is plenty for all."

Shocked, Scar stared at Loni.

Did I really hear him speak?

It was the first time he had ever heard Loni's voice.

Scar obeyed. And when he came back, he was allowed within the circle. Yet, there were conditions: every time he grew impatient, tried to rush or fight for what he thought should be his share, the barrier was raised against him...until he surrendered, and gentled.

Somehow, Loni did it...and wisely, Scar learned to respect this method. There was sufficient, so...Scar was content. Especially, when he finally got it in his head, they did not intend to deny him.

****

Loni had decided to trust Scar. He needed his help, and it was safer to take him with, than to leave him behind with Da and the women.

He chose after work to begin his project. The girls needed the rest, so Loni left Da guarding them, and the first evening, after the meal was over, he caught Scar by his arm, and led him away toward the drain bar-gate.

This first night was simply to orientate.

As his head topped the hole leading onto the ledge, and Scar's eyes went wide with the vision of the world above, Loni filled the man's mind with the images of what had happened to his brother. He didn't have to warn him farther.

Scar crawled gingerly, carefully to the edge of the ledge, and hesitantly peered over. Loni knew from mere sense, Scar fully expected to be grabbed by the Hydra.

He read also, in the mind of the man, the expectation that he, Loni, meant to do away with him, but at least, Scar no longer believed Loni or Gem had killed his twin.

Loni crept forward, to pull Scar back, but true to his training, Scar immediately cringed in fear. Loni waited until the man calmed, and was more confident to trust him, then Loni led Scar to the bridge. He placed a finger to his lips, and sent him a mental command.

"No sound," he cautioned, and Scar nodded.

The path was of boards held together with rivets, over metal tubes, with rails on the sides about waist high; it did not sway in the wind; was exceedingly firm, but always, there was the worry, the danger, of the predators: the Hydra, and far in the distance, what appeared to be dinosaurs. Their bellows resounded distinctly from afar, all the while the men inched forward.

Many fright-ridden steps later, the two arrived at the miniature dome-shaped structure atop the first tree. When they peered inside, they found it merely a shell, but it held piles of boards, rolls of transparent, paper-thin canvas, that appeared to be rain proof, and rails, as were used to construct the bridge, with the rivets, and tools to build all. There were also schematics, drawings of more domes and walkways. If you could not read the words, the diagrams were descriptive enough in themselves.

Loni was pleased. Apparently, someone had already planned the getaway he meant to set up. But, what had become of them? Had the Hydra done away with them?

****

The days that followed were busy; exhausting; and draining; filled with apprehension, and excitement. On one hand, what they were about, must not be discovered; on the other, it must appear, they were not lax at their duties. At first, their days were filled simply with gardening; the long nights, into the wee hours of morning, they built new structures out in the upper world.

After that, Scar and Loni hauled in the supplies, stealing them carefully, so that the fact they were missing would go unnoticed.

The first shed was still for storage. Here they put backpacks of seed packets, trays of seedlings, small grafting of fruit trees; bedding, blankets, various sizes of coveralls; soap, metal cooking containers...anything Loni felt they might need in the future.

All depended upon, whether they could get away unnoticed.

Scar understood to speak carefully, as they went about their secret duties, and never mention the project if others could hear. The one armed twin learned to obey Loni without question. His life, and that of his companion, depended upon it...the Hydra was a constant threat hovering in the background.

And so hesitantly, Loni and Scar, both, learned to trust each other.

At last, sometimes, Loni left Scar behind for a much needed rest, and took Da instead. The first night he did that, Loni was exceedingly nervous; he and Da returned much earlier than usual, but upon finding all sleeping, Loni was most relieved. After that, trust came easier.

Chapter 32

One night, when Loni and Scar returned, they found Da pacing, wringing his hands, beside himself in panic. Lydia sat beside Loni's mate, sobbing piteously. Gem was in labor!

It was not that either of the other two had never seen such a thing; but that they were caught in ugly memories, fearful, and uncertain what to do.

Loni didn't even bother washing up in the pool they had built for that purpose, at the side of the waterfall; he went direct to his tormented mate.

****

It wasn't easy for Loni to do two things at once; on the one hand, he needed to be at Gem's feet to catch the new born; on the other Gem needed his strength, but holding her hand to give it to her, kept him from helping the little one.

And then there was Lydia. She had completely lost it, sobbing as if Gem and the baby were going to die. But when Loni entered her thoughts, he realized the problem. She was thinking more of the babies she'd lost.

Perhaps, I can involve her somehow?

"Lydia," he shouted into her mind. "I need your help. Go to Gem's feet. Catch the baby."

Lydia stared at him, at first not comprehending; her sobs quieting, as the order sunk in; her body still shaking with the resulting hiccupping tremors. After more than one try, Loni finally got through to her. The younger woman wiped at her tears, and obediently, moved into place.

Loni looked about; saw Scar apparently asleep on his mat.

Good! He'll be no problem. But...where did Da go?

He sighed. Of all times for the boy to disappear.

Another contraction was assaulting his woman. Loni willed Gem his energy, so she could fight through it. Loni felt the weakness flood over him, as he traded vigor for limitation.

And then, Gem was pushing. Lydia was yelling excitedly:

"It's coming! I see its head!"

Suddenly, the feeble wail of a new born, from a distance; Loni realized he'd near passed out; giving too much of his life force. The man let go of Gem's hand, and went to cut the cord; and after that...deal with the afterbirth.

****

Scar recognized what was happening. He had often watched as cows and pigs gave birth, but...he had never seen a human do it. As Loni took control of the situation, Scar decided simply to observe, retiring to his own mat, where he lay down, feigning sleep, but covertly watching, one eye open, hidden by his folded arm.

The one armed twin noted when Da left. It seemed to Scar, the simple one was in such a state, he couldn't stay and watch. Also, Scar was quite certain Loni hadn't told Da to go; that man was too busy with the ministrations to his pregnant partner.

The tears Lydia was shedding told Scar another story. He had gathered enough, previously, to know the Physicians had taken her baby, and Lydia was mourning the loss of that young one; paralyzed into uselessness. More than likely, this new birthing was bringing back unpleasant memories.

While the twins were together Galar had often instigated torment of the animals. Because of that conditioning, such a scene as this, merely amused Scar. He lay there, enjoying the madness of the scene.

When the baby dropped from its mother, Lydia caught it; and Scar realized, he'd been wool gathering.

How was Lydia commandeered into helping?

He had missed something.

After the baby was freed of the cord, and swaddle wrapped, Loni gave the infant into Lydia's care. As he turned to clean up his mate, the younger woman cuddled the baby girl to her breast.

****

For so long, Lydia had ached, her nipples leaking hourly; her milk was full and ready, and the sound of the infant's cries made it flow. She opened the flap of her coveralls, and pressed the child against her swollen breast. The seeking, tiny-one nuzzled, and quickly latched on. Her hungry drawing soon eased Lydia's prolonged discomfort.

Lydia sighed, as if she had been given a reprieve.

Loni turned, and saw. Chuckled. To her mind alone, he commented:

"You haven't dried up! That's good. Between the two of you, my wee one will be well fed."

Tears sprang to Lydia's eyes.

He didn't scold; he approves.

Because of that, when Gem held out her arms for the baby, Lydia didn't mind giving it up. Gem too, seemed happy, smiling widely at her.

****

As she nursed her new born, hours later, Gem noticed how Scar sat across the camp, on his mat, scrutinizing her every move.

Lydia had gone back to her mat, asleep now, that she was at last more comfortable; Da, as yet, had not returned. Loni was asleep, also, lying just behind Gem's back.

She raised the infant to her shoulder, to burp the little one, and between the gentle pats, beckoned with her hand, for Scar to come near. The one armed twin inched like a dog across the dust of the center court, timidly, hesitant. With each encouraging wave, he moved closer, until he sat beside her on the bed.

Loni did not stir; he appeared more exhausted than the mother of the new one.

The baby was asleep now, content. Gem carefully eased her into the crook of Scar's arm, directing him on holding her safely, as she did so.

If I let him hold her, he should feel more included...

But Gem chose not to invade his thoughts. Perhaps if she had, what came after, might have been prevented.

****

Scar hadn't wanted to return the soft, cuddly bundle, but after much persuasion, he had given in. She, once more, slept next to her mother. He'd obeyed the woman dutifully, returning to his pad, but his mind objected. Also, he feared reprisal from Loni, if he showed disrespect to his woman.

Sometimes, Scar still felt, she was supposed to be his, but Loni had her now, so they must be sharing.

But, she gave me the baby! It is mine now! That's why she did it; to show me. It's up to me to see that it keeps safe...I think...up-side would be best. That's why Loni prepared the new houses.

It wasn't often Scar had to think for himself. It is no wonder, his decisions were flawed.

Quietly, he crept to the sleeping mat of the new family. As Gem had shown him, he eased the cocooned bundle into the crook of his arm. It squirmed, stretched, and grunted. He nearly dropped it, but then it settled down again. He stood, slowly inched away, then headed toward the down ladder.

But when he got there, he realized, having only one arm, he couldn't descend, couldn't take his burden with him. He needed something to help him carry his package. Scar decided, a fruit sack would be perfect. It hung over the neck, down his front, and left his hand free.

But they are kept in the storage shed, out in the orchards...have to put her down somewhere.

He wandered away from the campsite, seeking a safe place for his small package; where she would be comfortable, yet unseen. And his supposed delegated charge, slept on, oblivious, unaware, she was being stolen from her scrumptious meal provider.

Off, away, far back in the trees, he found what he sought; a pile of rocks, discarded while planting, and clearing a field. Scar stooped; lay the baby in the dirt. Then, one by one, he placed the rocks in a circle around the swaddled infant.

A finally touch; he placed the last large rock, like a roof, balanced on the others. It hid his self-appointed charge expertly from view. And, she...slept on.

Turning from the cairn, Scar fled.

Chapter 33

Da watched from above, as the scientist left the experimental lab. His baby girl was there, in an incubator, tubes running from the machine, around and inside, sticking out of the infant's nose, attached to a tiny foot; needles leading in to feed her, who knew what? Drugs?

I have to stop this! No more! But, I have to prevent them from coming in while I do it...need some kind of distraction...

He left his sentry position.

My little belly bump can't be worse off, while I go away to create the diversion that will save her life.

He slunk down the corridors leading away; hiding in corners and doorways when gowned, masked experimenters passed him, near inches away. They never even noticed him.

Da sought something, anything he could use; he knew not what at the moment. Then, there it was: the forbidden closet!

So often, Loni had cautioned Da, warned him never to go into one of these, and if he ever did so, he must never touch the things inside.

Loni had said, the chemicals, and cleaning agents inside had been brought across by the returning Physicians, stolen from the world from which Lydia and Gem came. These elements were poisonous, caused fumes, smoke, and...fire, if they were spilled together. Loni had been burned by such an acid; that was why he had no ears.

This would create the perfect diversion!

As Da entered, closed the door behind him, pulled the cord to light the overhead bulb, and tentatively gazed about, he thought on what else Loni had said: to take precautions...always!

All three walls were covered in shelving, from floor to ceiling, and each ledge was filled with appropriated contraband: towels and sheets; gowns and gloves; blankets; tubing, needles, and many more instruments Da could not identify, but at the moment, he sought only one specific thing.

And there, at the very top, he saw them!

They were piled high, all in disarray, as if thrown at random, no one caring about neatness.

Paper masks! They were meant to fit over the nose, and mouth, to protect against smell...and fumes...and things that were bad for you.

But Da couldn't reach them.

Then he spied the stool, hidden there beneath the bottom shelf, on the middle wall. He pulled it out, moved it over beneath the side wall, and mounted it, not realizing he must first lock the supports. He reached, barely caught what he was after, before he over balanced, and...fell, the whole unstable unit toppling on top of him.

For a second Da lay there, not hurt, but listening. No sound in the hallway.

At least he had his mask to cover his face!

As he stood, he hardly noticed the mess he had made; Da simply left the paper coverings strewn about him. He was too intent, and in a hurry, to get this business done.

After donning his hard won mask, Da searched around for what would fulfill what he really needed.

Deep in a far corner, where the shelves were more firmly fixed, Da found what he sought: a metal scrubbing bucket and mop, and...the canisters, boxes, and bottles of cleaning agents.

Now, for the next step!

He removed the mop; there was no need for that. Next he took down every bottle with liquid in it, and went to work.

What he wanted was enough smoke...or fumes, to fill the halls, and cause a panic among those working in this sector. If it was confined to one closet, it would take them awhile to determined where the odor, and smoke, came from. It would give him the time to set his small one free from the incubator.

Da emptied each bottle, one at a time, into the aluminum pail. Each seemed to run so slow, gurgling forth at a snail's pace. He became impatient, even before he had all of the first batch poured in. First bleach, then ammonia...and anything else available.

He could almost hear Loni scolding him in his head, even though he knew, Loni knew nothing of what Da was doing.

"Slow down," it seemed to say. "Plenty of time. When you rush, you make a mistake."

How many times had Loni said just that?

One after the other, Da watched the bottles empty.

He needed something to make it smoke; perhaps this canister? It read: Drano. And that did it! With a small puff of an explosion, the smoke started filling the air.

Da could smell it now, even through his mask. It was time to get out of there!

At least the fumes were rising; up toward the vent in the ceiling. But, the smoke was making it impossible to see; filling the small room, seeping under the door to the outside.

Can't stay! All done! This should do!

Da kicked the pail, and turned to the door. He didn't notice the splash, as the pail slid away. Acid splattered, on the floor, the paper face masks...and ignited a tiny spark against one.

Da opened the door carefully, peered hesitantly around the doorframe. All was clear; the corridor empty. He closed the door behind him, and fled.

But...with the small breeze created by the closing door, a draft fanned the small spark. The paper mask burst into flame, lighting the others. Not soon after, the room became a roaring inferno; before Da had even reached the other end of the hall.

Oblivious to what was developing behind him, Da pulled off his mask, tossed it away, and headed out, once again, to the experimental lab...and to the rescue.

****

The crying of a faint, panicked voice in his head brought Loni to full consciousness. Beside him, Gem woke with a start, at the same instant.

"Where is the baby?" she telepathed to him. "Does Lydia have her?"

But, when together they looked over to Lydia's mat, she was sleeping soundly, dead to the world. Next, their eyes went to Scar's corner.

He was gone!

As one, they shot to their feet.

Like tracking dogs, it wasn't hard for the pair to follow the mental print of their daughter. Her thoughts were basic, infantile...to be expected. She should not have even been in the position to call out to them. All the wee one demanded was: milk; her bottom dry; and a less uncomfortable, confining space.

Her cries were audible, as they neared her.

They were appalled at where, and how, she'd been hidden.

She screamed her indignation, as they lifted the rock roof from her cave. With obvious anger, Loni flung away the rocks of the ring surrounding their treasure.

He knew who had imprisoned the child; the why did not matter!

Gem, lifted the infant gently, cuddling her against her chest. Then baring her leaking breast, the mother nursed her child on the spot.

****

Da crept into the experimental lab, fearful of being detected. Warning sirens were sounding everywhere; apparently the distraction had worked, as no attendant was in evidence.

He went first to the incubator, to gaze lovingly at his belly bump. She was so small; tiny little toes and fingers, but...all there; the mouth sucking one thumb.

But, no time to dawdle.

Let's get this done!

Da moved to a nearby row of shelves. He'd seen what they contained when watching from above: diapers, towels and washcloths; a sort of wrapper thing that fit around your chest, tied at the back...or front, as you chose, so you could carry the infant from place to place. He had seen it used at other times.

He donned the wrapper carry-thing, tied it so his burden would be in front, then grabbed a diaper, and made for the incubator, again.

First thing, Da pulled the electrical plug powering the machine, and then all the tubes leading into it. The insistent beeping, that started the minute he unplugged, was drowned by the loud and persistent warning sirens. But now, he knew, he needed to hurry, before someone noticed and came.

He lifted the lid on the tiny bed; quickly removed the needle and tubing from her foot. As he pulled the tube from the baby's nose, she gagged, and went limp; the thumb she had been sucking lay abandoned beside her open gasping mouth. A moment later, she appeared not to be breathing at all, but Da had no time to think of that. All he wanted was to get her free.

Loni will fix her, if I can't. He couldn't fix Lydia...but, Gem did. She will fix my baby bump!

And Da thought no more about it.

He diapered the tiny bottom, glad the sides of the garment stuck to each other. He lifted, ever so carefully, and slid the wee creature inside his chest pack.

Then Da turned, and ran like the Hydra was chasing him.

****

When Scar rose to the top of the ladder, the empty sack hanging from his neck, prepared to carry the blue infant baby away with him, he found she was already back with her parents.

Finding an empty, and destroyed cairn, he knew immediately what had happened, and when he went back to the campsite to claim her, Scar found the baby, he felt had been given to him, asleep in Gem's arms.

It annoyed him, but he could wait.

He returned to his sleep pad, to lay down, but Loni would have none of it. At first sight of Scar, Loni shot to his feet. The wrath emanating from both the telepaths was palpable.

In a second, before Scar could sit, Loni had crossed the center of the camp area, and floored him with one solid punch, direct on his jaw.

To this point, Loni had never been aggressive or violent with Scar; his self control was ever at the forefront; patience never absent...until the perceived injury to his tiny, helpless infant. It was evident, this was Loni's breaking point; where he drew the line.

The blow had hit hard, with all the anger and frustration, building since Gem's kidnapping, behind it; even Loni had been unaware of this evidence of a seething loathing, smoldering beneath the surface.

As Scar struggled to regain his senses, he clearly understood the irate words in his head.

"Never, are you EVER to touch that baby again! Do you hear me? NEVER! You get away from here; stay away...until you learn! This is our child! No one takes it from us! It is not Galar's; not yours! Ours!"

With that said, Loni turned. His temper cooled, even as he returned to his mate.

But Scar didn't know that.

All the one armed twin knew was, he was no longer welcome. But...how many times had Galar said the same words? He would go away now...Galar always took him back again later...

But, I'll get even...just you wait.

Scar rose shakily to his feet, turned, picked up, and slung, his knapsack onto his back. Then, with evident temper, he stomped toward the ladder leading down.

And as Scar disappeared, had he looked up, instead of down, he might have seen Da...descending from above, a listless soft bundle in a pouch around his chest.

Chapter 34

Loni was watching the ladder; he wanted no more surprises. He expected Scar to come back with a weapon, and attack. What he was unprepared for was to see Da, first his legs, and belly, then the small lifeless burden wrapped around his middle, and finally, the despondent expression on the dark one's features; Da coughing uncontrollably, as he stepped out into their camp grounds.

His patience gone, Loni sent the thought more sharply than he planned.

"What have you done, Da? What have you got there?"

Loni went quickly into the simple one's mind, and knew in an instant the conditions surrounding. He relaxed somewhat, as he realized there would not be chase given for some time, if at all.

"She won't breathe!" Da thought with panic. "I think she is dead."

"Your baby?" Loni questioned. "This one is Lydia's?"

Da nodded; tears in his pleading eyes.

****

During the ruckus with Scar, Lydia had feigned sleep. No amount of disorder penetrated much into her listless depression. Her babies were both gone; the one back with its father; the second, the Physicians had murdered.

What reason do I have to take any interest in what is going on about me?

Lydia knew, something had happened with Gem's little girl. When the pair returned, Loni was so protective, shadowing Gem and her infant, as if all in the world about them were their enemies.

But Gem has HER baby! It isn't dead!

Lydia knew it was alive; she could hear it suckling noisily at Gem's breast.

She couldn't help it; she felt jealous. As much as Gem was willing to share, that little one did not replace the one Lydia had lost.

She remained quiet through all the following disturbance; the ensuing fight between Loni and Scar, not reacting, whether in sympathy to either or not; remaining immobile, but listening, though she was not privy to the telepathic message Loni projected. Lydia was actually relieved, when the one armed man stormed away in anger.

Scar had always elicited a feeling of unease in her.

In the ensuing silence that followed, after the man left, Lydia had almost drifted off to sleep again. When Da came down the upward ladder, from the nursery area, situated to the left and above the falls, she started awake. He was gasping for breath, coughing , as if he'd been in a smoke filled room...or crying, or maybe both. Da was moaning and groaning over the bundle in his arms.

Lydia hadn't seen him since before Gem's baby was delivered, but in her emotionless state, she felt little enthusiasm at his return; nor sympathy. She remained docile, as if slumbering, on their pad.

As no words were spoken aloud, she had to figure out what was transpiring. It took her awhile to realized, they were fussing over a second infant.

Da brought another baby? Why?

And then that sixth sense kicked in, her mother sense, and it brought her shooting to a sitting position on her bed.

Without being told, Lydia understood...Da had found her little one, and...brought it home to her.

Before they reached her sleeping place, Lydia was beside the men, guiding them toward it. As Da clumsily tried to undo the wrapper around his burden, she was impatiently fighting against him, forcing away the cloth, to reveal the limp form within. Expressing verbally, Lydia gave stuttering voice to all the others were feeling.

"Oh, oh; my tiny, little one; my dear, precious baby. Where, oh where, did you find it?"

It would not have mattered if the child was really the one aborted from her womb; it could have been any child. She would have taken it in trade of the one missing. But, Lydia knew, beyond a doubt...this was her infant!

The golden brown color of the skin; a cross between Da's dark, and her own white. The doll-like face, resembling her child left behind, even to the bow-shaped lips; the dark hair. Oh, there was no disputing it...THIS WAS HER BABY! She recognized it.

When it was finally free, Lydia snatched the minute creature up in her arms, cuddled it against her bosom, but...it remained limp and unresponsive.

Why is it so still?

As realization hit her, Lydia cried out in anguish.

"W...why? Why? W...would you bring me a dead baby?"

Her tone was so filled with remorse; hopeless agony, it smote the hearts of those who heard. Even in mind thought, the rending accusation came across as rebuke.

And though Lydia clearly heard Loni's thoughts telling her otherwise, she refused to believe, or to take his comfort.

Then, Gem joined them, clutching her own new born, as if she feared to leave it alone on the other mat, less it be stolen. Gem tried to force Lydia to trade infants, so she could do what was necessary, as she had done, not so long ago, for the mother.

But Lydia was not about to give up what had just been returned to her. She had her baby back; they were not taking it away again!

****

Gem gave her wee one to its father. She would have to do the healing without Loni's energy support.

With her hands finally free, she fought Lydia for the other child. The woman was strong, and desperate, not understanding that they meant to help. Her unreasoning fear was all that filled her mind. Da attempted to help, but to no avail.

At risk to his own child, one handed, Loni endeavored to pull the dying baby from Lydia's grasp. As a last resort, he mentally slugged her. Lydia dropped in her tracks, in a dead faint.

And Gem was free to heal.

****

Lydia opened her eyes to the uncomfortable pinching, drawing of a suckling infant at her breast...and a throbbing headache.

She was laying on her mat, the baby cradled against her. Da sat at her back, hovering protectively, as if he dared not leave his family out of his sight. Loni crouched on one knee, in front of Lydia, while Gem stood a ways behind him, once more holding her own infant, and nursing, also.

When Loni noticed Lydia was awake, with an apparent throbbing headache, which he had caused, he reached gently forward, touching her temple.

Immediately, all discomfort vanished; Lydia breathed a sigh of relief, settled back. The world seemed less chaotic, now.

As she pondered the events that had gone before; those she remembered, Lydia realized what Gem had done for her baby, and how she, Lydia, had been preventing the implementation of such needed healing. Ashamed, thankful, and overwhelmed, she began to cry.

"It's okay, Lydia...all okay, now," Gem's crooning voice in her head attempted to soothe. "We are all okay, now."

But Lydia could not stem the flow of tears; tears of gratefulness...and relief...and overpowering appreciation...for this second chance at motherhood.

But then, as other actuality swarmed in, doubts pushed away happiness.

"How will we hide the little ones?" she asked with dread, brushing frustratingly at her remaining tears. "How will we keep them secret from the overseers and the Physicians? The babies are...female!"

Chapter 35

As he climbed away, Scar's smoldering wrath exploded; if he'd had two arms, he would have been throwing things. He descended away, far down deep, passing the garden level; the cattle pens; the chicken coops; the breeding pens for meat sources: pigs; goats; dogs, even cats. Down into the bowels, he went past the vats of manure, used for fertilizer on the gardens; the recyclers ...to the very guts of the huge domes.

Yes, there was more than one dome, all connected beneath the abandoned surface world, in the honeycombed caverns, that had existed for centuries, before they were used in this way. Like ants, his ancestors had burrowed beneath, to build a safe haven against nuclear war, and the resulting poisonous atmosphere they had created. The system had one flaw; if something drastic were to happen, down in the lower regions of one dome...an explosion, perhaps, the interconnection between all, would bring about a chain reaction, destroying the lot, perhaps even the entire planet.

All Scar needed to do, was figure out the how!

Finally Scar's temper cooled. On a grated ledge over the recycling vats, he sat down to think.

The one armed man intensely missed his brother; his dead twin had been the schemer; the brains of the partnership. Galar could be devious; dream up the most horrific punishments. Scar merely followed, but seldom did he not enjoy the results.

Remembering his brother, caused a curious resentment to surface. The very fact that the twins had always been the outcasts of this society, reasonably, generated first, an overwhelming loneliness, but also, today, gave birth to an unexpected bitterness.

What gave them the right to force us to work in the slaughter house? Just because we were unlike them?

And then his thoughts went to his present situation. His companions were ostracized, too. Loni because he had no ears; Da, because he couldn't understand. And their females were different, also...not normal, at least...much like he was.

Scar shivered at the realization. He was not alone, after all!

But, Flaw/Loni had just cast him out of the group!

Only for a little while. Galar always takes me back; Loni will do the same.

Perhaps, he shouldn't have touched the small one?

But...Loni's she gave it to me! Didn't she?

It was so very puzzling.

Maybe, she only meant me to hold it? She did ask for it back...

****

For a long time Scar sat reasoning. His mad turned eventually away from his fellow workers, to their shared injustices.

The others were forced to constantly work in the gardens; heavy, back breaking work, but...decidedly better than in the slaughter house or cattle pens, and easier than rendering and the kitchens. Scar had actually been enjoying crop planting and harvest; life with the gardeners had been most pleasant.

To be vengeful toward them seemed wrong.

The government; the ones who enslave us, are the real offenders...those   taking   advantage;   using us...experimenting on us!

But what could be done against THEM?

He, Loni, and Da had built a new place outside. It wouldn't be wrong to use it...but, if he didn't do something to prevent them, the overseers would follow him out...and spoil that place, as they had done the one below.

No! I have to prevent that!

How?

The next thought came, as if someone had written it in his mind.

The recyclers!

****

The huge vats were filled with chemicals; the pipes leading out gigantic, going in all directions...one blockage would cause a back up; would result in the explosion of the whole unit.

But, Scar wouldn't stop at just one!

He went to the tool shack first. Scar still had the fruit sack he'd taken to carry the baby; he also had his backpack at his back. Inside the storage room, he found much that would   be   useful: crowbar;   pipe   wrenches;   timers, and...explosives.

He filled the fruit sack with many things...

****

It was now all over except the explosions. Scar had flattened or closed off more than one pipe leading away from the machines. Those were mostly the smaller pipes, but that was just to begin the sabotage. He had also placed numerous timers, attached to charges, on each machine.

They were timed to detonate one after the other, to begin in approximately five hours; if one failed, the others would still follow at intervals. He hoped he had plenty of time to make it back up to the surface; then he would live in the upper world.

But...he had one stop to make, first. Scar wanted meat in his new world.

****

Scar first went to the rendering plants. Removing his backpack, he emptied it of his toiletries; his cup; bowl, etc. They had stored extras in the first storage dome in the village above; there was no need for him to take his.

From around the processing area, he gathered sausage, cut roasts, and raw chicken parts. Surprisingly, while he filled his backpack with them, he avoided anything made of human meat. He had learned well from Loni.

That man had told him, the reason the overseers were so dangerous, mad and aggressive. They were human meat eaters!

After shouldering this burden, Scar moved to the breeding stalls. He came first to the pig pens. Quickly, from a sow with a litter a week old, he scooped, from among those to choose from, three tiny piglets; one of black, a male; and two, one spotted pink and black, another pure white, each female, stuffing them together down deep into the fruit sack. The lack of air inside, made the squealing piglets quiet, and grow still. He then went about the pens and stalls, setting all others free: goats; sheep, cows and pigs; even the dogs and cats. Some followed him; others were more hesitant, taking their time, even when they realized they were free. He stepped around the milling animals, heading for the bird coops.

Here, Scar found the incubators of tiny chicks growing beneath the heat lamps. He stuffed in as many as the upper half of the sack would hold, hoping among them was both male and female. And so began the formation of his future farming endeavor.

He then set all the other birds free: ducks; geese; turkeys and grouse, chickens of every kind, that had been gathered, and brought through the transportation portal over the years. Most were unable to fly; they scattered away, among the rest of the menagerie, none knowing which way to go.

Fleetingly, Scar wondered where everybody was; why no one was around to stop him. His ulterior reasoning was to deprive the elite of their privileged meal fare, but he also had another, more devious, purpose in mind...

****

Loaded near beyond his ability to carry; the food at his back; the baby animals at his front, the one armed thief headed down through the sewer, where he would eventually get out , and up the ladder to the world above. His hope was the animals and poultry, he had set free, would follow, and distract the deadly monster, whose lair he must pass, feeding it, giving it its fill, before he arrived...so Scar could safely pass by.

Squealing little piglets moved on passed him, running hopelessly to their death, some stopping to gorge on tidbits in the running, fuming, rivulet beneath their feet, prolonging the inevitable. A large heifer ran by, the slope causing her to trip. she went down, then head over hoof, rolling like a giant miss-shaped package, eventually going over the shelf into the abyss beneath.

And then appeared the Hydra, its many heads swaying, one huge, fanged jaw opening, to catch the unfortunate cow in mid fall. It then, disappeared from sight to enjoy such a large, unexpected repast.

Scar breathed a sigh of relief; his distraction was effective. He took the shelf, moving over and across it, until he reached his destination: the ladder going upward. When he came to the rung-ladder he, and Loni, had so often traversed, he was shocked to find, he was not alone. Following, just behind him, determined, and more intelligent than most, also, fearless, was an obstinate nanny goat.

Ignoring her, Scar began the climb; for him, each bar difficult, with only one arm. One rung at a time, the man went up, and behind him, imitating his action, the goat found it easier, as it had four legs.

Let the dumb thing follow, then! It will give me milk.

What Scar did not expect, when he, and his shadow, reached their destination, and gained the outside ledge, behind the she goat, five offspring followed, as determined to go after mother's milk, as their parent had wanted freedom. Each had negotiated the rungs with unfailing fortitude.

And so, Scar truly had the makings of a future cattle farm.

Chapter 36

Loni sat on his mat deep in thought. They had to leave, beyond a doubt...and immediately.

This would be the beginning of a new life...

He would begin by getting out the two little ones he had, and of course, Gem, Da, and Lydia. Later, he might come back for other infants...or older boys...as they were prepared to handle them.

That would be a twofold endeavor: the work crew, and...future partners. Loni would be very careful whom he chose...

The surface would be their responsibility; they would be charged with repopulating that new upper world. For that, they would need at least two younger males. His daughter, and Da's, would bring about a second generation.

Dare I take more babies from this genetic gene pool? What if they tend toward violence, like the overseers?

He couldn't discipline a much larger group; Scar proved difficult enough. But with Gem's help...maybe, they could guide a two parent family...

For now, first things first, he would need to set up a barrier protected food supply; fruit trees needed planting; plots required preparation, and vegetables must be seeded. Until that produced, it was necessary to take a fresh food supply; they would need to steal it from in here. That meant, they would be going back and forth...

But...they couldn't pilfer what they needed for long...someone would get wise.

It's time for action; the rest will work itself out!

"Da," he thought projected. "Come. Bring your backpack; empty it first."

****

Gem had been following Loni's mental musings, agreeing with them fully, but she had some plans of her own. As soon as the men went to load up on fresh food, she rose from the mat, and started after them, intending to go above, not toward the fruit stands.

The little ones have needs, also...

"Lydia, stay here," she ordered verbally. "I'll be back shortly."

Gem had her thoughts on the future, too, but, just not as far distant, as were Loni's plans. She knew the infants wouldn't stay small for long. Beyond six months, they would need different garments, and...they could not subsist on breast milk alone. They would need to be introduced gradually to ground meal, and pureed fruit, and vegetables, as their teeth came in.

While visiting the Physician's offices, when they had given her the supplement, that Loni had immediately thrown away, she had seen the large pharmacy, and storage area, for the infants and mothers. It contained a huge store of baby food, and like paraphernalia.

With her baby held close against her shoulder, Gem caught up her backpack, climbed the ladder heading up, then proceeded down the corridor leading to the area she sought.

I definitely need a snuggly like Lydia has, to free up my hands...and boxes of dried pabulum...jars of puree. Lydia's baby is older by more than two months, so we'll need this fresh supply quick enough.

She was aware, it had all come from her home planet; pilfered by those who worked on the wards there. That way, she was confident, it was all safe...even the pureed meats.

But...are the medications? Baby cough syrup; salves; fever drugs...maybe?

There was no telling what the climate outside on the surface would be like for a young child, nor what future infections might develop. It was safest to use conventional methods of repair, where ever possible...less drain on the healer's system, then doing it, out right mind regeneration every time. Their bodies needed to learn to heal themselves.

In here the atmosphere is controlled...best be prepared for all eventualities.

She stuffed her empty backpack with all she thought of use.

Now for baby clothes...and diapers. Towels are just too harsh on their tender bottoms.

As she planned, Gem was so intent on her appropriation, she did not realize, behind her, Lydia had disobeyed her suggestion.

****

Lydia quickly slid her little one carefully down the front of her snuggly, then safely bound it to her breast.

No way are you leaving me behind again, all by myself!

Grabbing her backpack, Lydia slung it to her back, and hurried after Gem. But Gem had a head start, yet Lydia was certain she had headed up, not down. It wasn't long, and Lydia had lost sight of the other woman.

At the top of the ladder, Lydia turned the opposite way, the wrong way. The hall was filled with smoke, and an odorous stench that took away your breath, but she felt this was the direction Gem had gone, so she doggedly continued on.

Soon Lydia was coughing violently, gasping for air. With the edge of the baby's wrap, she attempted to protect her own mouth and nose, but her eyes were watering, as well. At least, deep inside the snuggly, her infant seemed protected.

Where ever did Gem go? Why is she so determined to come up here, anyway?

Lydia met no one; it appeared all personnel had vacated the premises.

Need to get a mask to protect my lungs...

****

Loni and Da had not been gone long. With their backpacks loaded down with fruit, beverages, and other edible necessities, Loni stepped from the ladder, Da following.

The older man immediately realized the camp site was empty, and his mind reached out in panicked search for the thoughts of his mate. His first notion was that Galar had somehow survived, or that Scar had returned, and one, or the other, or both, had stolen Gem again.

With relief, he found her mind; Gem was perusing the shelves of medications in the upper maternity levels.

Why didn't I think of that? Of course, we'll need such things!

"They are getting baby supplies, up above." Loni showed Da in his head. Of course, though he hadn't seen them both, Loni assumed the women were together. "You find Lydia, get her out, and meet us at the ledge on the outside...by the crossing to the new village."

Da nodded understanding, and took off, ahead of Loni, up the ladder.

For a moment, Loni lingered.

Is there anything important we are leaving behind?

No. Not really. No need to return.

****

After filling her pack with expropriated contraband, Gem felt curious. She desired to see what the facility looked like; where the birthing women were kept, and...the other babies.

Where are the younger males raised?

For the first time, she noticed how the air was filled with a slight haze of smoke. From a nearby shelf, she grabbed up a surgical mask, and put it on, then stuffed a handful of the same masks into the front of the snuggly that now held her baby.

It wasn't long, and she found a room filled with cribs. Each one contained a sleeping boy child, not more than a year old. Her heart went out to these young ones, but she knew she couldn't save all of them.

Maybe...I could just take one of them...

But, she could never carry everything...and the room was now so filled with smoke, she felt sudden fear for those left behind.

Over in a corner, she spied a play area. Among the stacked, and scattered blocks, the dozens of stuffed animals, and squeaky toys, stood a small two-seater tin wagon. It was old, rusted, and dilapidated, but it would do.

Gem made for it, but as she pulled it forward, and it complained violently, a fear struck her.

What if the noise draws the attention of the attendants?

Looking around, Gem frowned. She hadn't seen a single caregiver the whole time.

Where are they all? There is obviously a fire in here some place...why doesn't the pump system clear away the smoke? And, where are the firefighters?

It dawned on her, then, the fire and emergency men had been unavailable, ever since the flood in their lodgings, way before Galar had taken her.

These babies will die of smoke inhalation...they haven't just left them to die? Surely not!

All the more reason to take those she could...

Tugging the squeaking wagon, she went along the rows.

Whom to choose; who to let die?

Gemma shivered with dread. It was a terrible task, playing god.

A very small boy caught her eye. His skin was coal black; a fine feather of curl covered the top of his head. He was balled into a fetal position, as if trying to escape the inevitable. Gemma had never seen such a tiny year old.

As she lifted him, placed him in the wagon, blanket and all, he hardly stirred. She covered his mouth, and nose, with one of the surgical masks. At least, he was still breathing.

She couldn't save them all...but, maybe, just one more...

In a far corner of the room, a single crib stood by itself. Gem stopped short, drawing in a breath in shock.

****

Da discovered Lydia right where he had found their infant daughter. She was staring morosely into the little torture chamber, the incubator, where the Physicians had held captive their tiny belly-ball.

Why has she come here? Does she want to see what was done? Would she rather put our baby back?

But, purely by accident, Lydia had come upon the containment pod. She appeared mesmerized by the empty bed, with its tubes, and cord hanging loose, and as she gazed into the empty container, Lydia had suddenly realized its purpose. She drew her infant more closely against her, as if, now, she felt more qualified to protect her from any future damage.

Da tugged at her arm; Lydia jerked as if struck. Finally realizing he was there, she went into his arms, and he embraced her in the firm hug she so desperately needed.

By the time they pulled apart, they were both coughing uncontrollably. Da reached to a nearby shelf, pulled down a handful of surgical masks, put one on Lydia, another on himself, and stowed the rest in his pack. Then he led her away, out another door.

Chapter 37

Gem stared at the infant sitting in the crib; it was like looking at a miniature Loni, except that this two year old had delightful, tiny, shell-shaped ears. His skin was the same pale white-blue; the eyes were turquoise, hair a curly white-blond. The boy sat there, staring back at her, as if he could see right into her mind.

Her immediate reaction was to close her thoughts from him.

And suddenly, Loni stood right there beside them.

"He looks just like me," Loni marveled, projecting both his thoughts, and his shock. "They've been experimenting with mother's genes; they must have grown him..."

They both cringed in revulsion at the very thought.

What an awful thing to do!

But the little boy had followed their silent communiqué. His immediate reaction was to think, rejection. His soulful eyes filled with tears, and he inched away, to the back wall of the crib.

"Oh, no!" cried Gem. "You are not the bad one. They were wrong, in what they did with you..."

The tiny boy sighed, reached his arms out, and up toward them. Mirroring tears filled Gem's own eyes, as she picked him up, and folded him against her.

She fitted him with a mask, before she made to place him in the wagon. As Gem leaned forward, the small boy patted questioningly at the bump inside her pouch.

My...little girl.

He grinned broadly, and allowed her to set him down. When she placed the sleeping, smaller, black boy in his arms, he was quite willing to hold him tightly to keep him safe.

As they passed a shelving unit, Loni grabbed a handful of surgical face protectors. Both he and Gem began fitting the smaller ones with the masks, The two young ones, Gem's baby, and the black child, were already quite lethargic.

The little blue-skinned boy seemed to understand the reasoning behind their actions; he had submitted willingly to the imprisoning of his nose and mouth.

As Loni finished securing the mask to the second boy, Gem forced another into his hand for himself. He quickly donned it, then, took the handle to pull the wagon.

****

With the wagon full of the two toddlers, and both Loni and Gem burdened down with loaded backpacks, Gem carrying her baby, as well, they knew they could not go straight down the ladders. They had to find another way out, so they travelled parallel, out along the corridors, through the lounge area of the holding quarters for the waiting pregnant women.

To Gem's dismay, even here, the air was thick with smoke and fumes.

"What is causing all the smoke in the air? Why doesn't the ventilation system filter it away?"

Loni answered her questions direct to her mind, as was their usual way of communication.

"Da started a fire, as a distraction; that's gotten out of hand. It was a chemical fire, and you know the firefighters have been nonexistent since our unit flooded. There is no one who knows how to fight this."

"But shouldn't the system take care of that on its own?"

"It's trying, but...I think instead of thinning the concoction, it spread the vapors all through these upper floors. It's gone from room to room, filling the air with poison..."

"My gosh, Loni! That will kill everyone! Especially the infants, back there in the cribs..."

"We can only carry so many, right now," Loni reasoned. "Maybe we can come back a second time...get some more..."

"They'll all be dead by then...does Da realize what he did in here?"

"Not likely; won't help to scold; he's too simple to understand."

They entered a delivery room, and Gem realized why they had not been challenged so far. The fumes had incapacitated the adults, already.

Slumped across his patient, a surgeon was out cold. So was the mother, and...the child she had just recently delivered. Gem thought they were merely unconscious; they would survive.

But, Loni disagreed with her observation.

"They are not simply unconscious," he stated in silent regret. "All are dead..."

Gem shuddered, and hurried past the scene at a run. The wagon, Loni pulled, complaining violently all the way.

Why does this thing have to make so much noise? It grates on my nerves...

In another room, they found women in various stages of pregnancy. Some had been walking off their labor pains, and had slumped lifeless against the wall, then slid to the floor. Others lay on sofas, but all had their eyes closed, no longer breathing.

"Dear lord! What could be that deadly?" Gemma demanded. "What did Da use? Where did he get something that lethal?"

"From the janitorial cupboard...he threw everything together..."

"We need to get down from here...out of here! Now! Or we'll save none of them."

Loni agreed with her urgent assessment.

"You take the handle," he ordered. "I'll lift from the back end. We'll be able to go faster."

Switching positions, they quickly found a ladder going down.

****

The next room Da and Lydia entered was a second nursery, for those under a year. Each crib held a tiny sleeping boy, and the room was empty of adults.

At first glance, the infants appeared to be sleeping, but the room was so filled with smoke you could barely see, and Lydia quickly realized the small boys were asphyxiating, some were coughing hoarsely in their sleep.

Horrified, Lydia ran to a shelf, caught up a snuggly, similar to the one in which she carried her child, moved quickly to Da, and tied it to his chest. For only a moment did she hesitate, then grabbing up a small Asian child, enclosed him securely down deep in the carrier at Da's front.

Da caught the idea of what she was attempting. First he grabbed surgical face masks, then one at a time, he put the shielding on two small dark haired boys, raised one in each arm, and turned.

In the mean time, Lydia had caught up a fourth infant, holding it against the swell of her entombed baby girl on her chest. Regrettably, she forgot to take the time to fasten a facemask on the child in her arms, even though he was gasping and choking for breath.

Together, the two adults, with their burden of infants, ran for a nearby down ladder. Two adults were only able to rescue these five small ones, as Da carried a pack of foodstuffs on his back, and Lydia didn't take the time to grab another snuggly.

The other occupants of the room, unhappily, were left to die.

****

Gem was trembling visibly, as she inched down the sewer that led past the slaughter house. Loni watched her memory plague her; thoughts of the atrocities she had suffered at the hands of Galar...

Loni pushed the wagon forward, forcing her to hurry more rapidly.

A chicken fluttered by.

Vaguely, he wondered where all the live animals beside them had come from, and how they had gotten free. Other thoughts puzzled him also...

What has become of Da? Has he found Lydia?

Loni had no time to search for their minds.

A pig and a goat moved along with the wagon.

What became of Scar?

Is Scar responsible for setting these cattle free? If so...why?

Always, Loni was suspicious of the one armed man's motives.

What possible purpose could be served, to send all these livestock to their deaths? It will attract the Hydra...is that it? So we can't get to the above settlement?

When they reached the first shelf, at the bottom of the sewer drain, they met up with Da and Lydia. It was obvious they had also been in the infant dorms.

Chapter 38

In his opinion, Da had way too much to carry. Before they went along the ridge, Loni decided to distribute the loads more evenly.

He and Gem, each, had been trying to carry one end of the wagon, but every once in a while, they had to set it down. The wheels were unstable, and squealed atrociously; it was pointless to take the thing further, besides, they couldn't lift it up the ladder all the way to the above world.

Gem caught up the small black boy, and that left Loni with only the two year old blue-skinned toddler.

Loni felt he was stronger than Da, so he had the other man remove both the backpack, and the snuggly. Loni donned the second backpack over his chest, and fitted the second snuggly, and child to Lydia's back. That freed Da to carry the two boys he still had. Lydia now carried two infants each in a snuggly, one at her front; the other in back, and one small boy in her arm.

Gem had enough with a backpack of infant supplies, her infant, and the small black child in her arm. Now, Loni was the one over burdened: two loaded backpacks, and a two year old.

Balancing carefully, they sidestepped across the ridge until they got to the ladder going upward. Here Loni separated the pairs. He sent Lydia up first. She didn't know the way, but was willing, when she understood it would be all straight up.

Next, Loni put Gem. He felt, if nothing else, the women would escape with some of the children. He sent Da next.

Da was having a hard time, with two little boys, who had come awake, and were squirming in his arms. He inched upward slowly, Loni following behind.

****

Lydia made the mistake of looking back. There, silently hovering above Da was a creature out of a nightmare. Snake-like, with many a long slender neck, dripping jaws, and frightful red eyes, the many headed creature wove to and fro, just waiting a chance to grab a small morsel from an inattentive adult rescuer.

Lydia screamed, loud and long...and let go of the small boy in her arms.

Below her, Gem looked up toward the sound, noticed the falling infant...and then, the Hydra.

She was quick, but not as swift as the beast. One snake-like head, on a long skinny neck, reached out. The jaws opened, and deftly caught the infant in freefall, but...it only snared the edge of the blanket wrapped around him, not any part of the actual child, and so...he hung there in mid air, suspended, waiting...to drop, again.

A red beam of light shot out from Gem's eyes. Like an errant laser, it sought its mark. When it found the throat, like a sharp knife, it cut away the head of the beast. But there were many other heads swaying behind the injured neck. The jaws of the severed head opened, releasing the boy, his wrap came undone. Both detached head, and naked baby went plummeting down, seemingly in slow motion.

Loni, beneath Gem, came into play. From his eyes, he shot forth a beam of blue light, toward the falling infant. Surrounded in blue haze, its fall stopped; for a second, he remained suspended, then slowly floated toward Loni's arms. The two year old already there, opened his arms, as if he knew exactly what the adults meant to accomplish. He caught the smaller boy, and held tight.

"Move Da!" Loni shouted to Da mentally. And the others, also, heard the thought command. "Get to the top, before someone else is taken! We can't fight it continually."

Moaning, her screams silenced, Lydia started to obey; Gem hesitating a mere second before following. Both Da, and Loni were too exposed. She didn't want to leave them unprotected.

And the Hydra wasn't finished. It was both angry, and cheated of a meal.

As Lydia made it over the top ridge, the beast struck again.

Da was the target, and this time, the monster dove for his legs. The two wriggling infants in his arms made the rising difficult. One skinny neck moved past his face, but it was merely to distract. A second head swept across his knees, and suddenly, Da hung there, one arm clinging to the ladder rung, the other trying to hold both the squirming boys. Da felt nothing...but, from the knees down, his feet were already missing.

He couldn't go up or down; one effort to grab the next rung, and all would fall.

Gem had gained the top of the ladder, but there was no lightening her load. She still had the sack of supplies at her back. She carefully lay the tiny black infant, from her arms, on the rock shelf, and rolled him toward Lydia. The woman quickly caught up the child, and cuddled him close.

But Gem still carried her own infant in the snuggly, which was not easily unfastened. Gem decided to keep it so, and peering over the edge, lying on her side, she did her best to help those below.

Da's grip was slackening; his strength giving way. From his extremities, he was bleeding profusely, and beginning to feel the pain. The Hydra had backed off to swallow the tidbit it had acquired.

Gem knew there was no hope for Da; he was as good as dead. Her beam shot out again, but this time in blue. From Da's arm, she snatched the first dark haired infant, levitating him upward toward her. And as she was occupied, the Hydra returned.

****

Loni was certain he had no future; with what was happening above him, he was powerless to help. Da was already lifeless; the second child would go with him, unless...

Loni's arms were full; he was loaded with full backpacks, front and back; couldn't even slip them off. His energy was fading, as well.

Loni rolled to the side, the children in his arms against the rock. He shot a red beam to the eyes of the nearest snake head, hoping merely to distract. He could do little more. And as Da fell past him, Loni switched to the blue levitation beam, encompassing the last infant in Da's arm. Just at that moment, the Hydra dropped to dive for the body of Da.

The second dark haired boy hung suspended, but Loni's energy quickly gave out. Regretfully, the man let the child go, and it fell, slowly revolving, over and over, as it plunged into the chasm below. Loni moaned aloud at the loss, but he had no more mental energy; he couldn't have held him, and levitated him to Gem...and she was busy saving the other.

He looked up, and saw, all the rest were safe.

****

Just as Loni made it over the top of the ladder on to the ridge, off in the distance, a loud detonation shook the ground. As he lay there, gasping for breath, exhausted, trying to puzzle out the cause for the noise, a second blast rent the air, causing the earth beneath his feet to shiver and shake; rocks to tumble; the whole ledge to move.

Horrified, Loni realized what was happening.

"We have to get off of here," he projected in panic to the others resting about him. "The whole underground is exploding. Someone has set off a charge. Get across the bridge."

As exhausted as he, Gem rolled to her side, and sat up. The pack was still attached, so was her baby, and she had the rescued dark haired child, as well. She could no longer carry the little black infant.

Lydia solved that. With her own in the snuggly, and another infant at her back, she lifted the small black boy, and started across the bridge to the first storage shed.

Gem followed; Loni after, running as fast as he could, with two packs, and two boys in his arms. The ground shook beneath their feet; a third explosion...and then, the unthinkable...the Hydra had slipped through the sewer to the outer ledge...and was back.

Chapter 39

Loni never realized what had happened until later. The blue skinned two year old was looking over his shoulder one minute; he stiffened, and shortly after went limp.

Behind, the little boy had seen the Hydra rise; he tensed. He had watched the minds of the adults, as they both had used the levitation beam and the defense, and like those of his kind, learned quickly. But being as young as he was, his power was limited.

From his young eyes, he shot his first defense beam. The red laser-like weapon found its mark; the eyes of the furious monster behind. Not expecting a challenge from the fleeing prey, it was surprised, halted, blinded immediately. It had backed off, and dropped back to its den in retreat.

****

Loni wondered, in all the fighting, if unnoticed by him, the small boy he held, had somehow been injured. However, as he labored across the bridge behind Gem, he had other things to worry about. The slats and rails were quickly giving way beneath his feet.

"Keep going! Keep going," he ordered telepathically. "We can't stay here!"

But though the damage stopped at the first tree dome, all of them ran on.

Until, that is, they came to the last dome house on the distant horizon.

The women stopped short, and Loni ran into them.

"What's wrong?" he probed from Gem.

Panting, she answered him.

"Listen! Oh, you can't hear..." Gem pointed to their destination.

Scar, Da, and Loni had built a village in the tree tops; twelve units in all. The outer core was mostly filled with storage; the farther away ones, in the center, were meant for family units. Lydia had followed the path, the bridges joining each, to the very outer empty dome.

And as Loni listened in, with the ears of the others, he now heard the most god awfully clamor imaginable. Goats were bleating, pigs squealing and grunting; chickens squawking...as if the shed was a farmyard full of a living menagerie.

Loni laughed. In that instant, he knew, he had found Scar.

Epilogue:

Gem called this upper world Azure Blue. It would never do to call it Earth! She hoped it would never come to that: rape, and greed, and always warring.

It was night now, as she rocked her small girl in her arms, nursing her. Across, in a second chair, Lydia slept, grieving still for Da, but content, with her own infant in her arms.

They had managed to get all the boys to sleep, and it was calming to cuddle quietly, now, with their girls.

They had lost one other small boy...besides Da, and the baby boy, that had died in the attack by the Hydra. Only six children remained: two tiny girls; four boys, three under the age of one, and...one two year old.

That blue skinned boy had finally opened his eyes a couple hours after they were settled in. His memories had enlightened them as to how he had tried to save Loni. As small as he was, so very young, he had discovered the purpose of a male defender. Always afterward, in the future, would he protect those younger, smaller, and weaker than he.

The other little soul they had lost, the one Lydia had forgotten to mask, had breathed his last, just after they had finally found sanctuary. Both she, and Loni, had been too exhausted to heal him. It was grievous, but each must go on again. Now, they had the task to minister to those still living.

Gem couldn't deny it was a miracle they had all come through it. Surely there was a God who had governed their paths; He'd reached down and taken care of each of them. Anyone who said it wasn't so was blind. The timing was too perfect...even the supplies taken out, and the number who had survived, right down to Scar and his meat supply.

At this moment, the men were making a barrier of thorn bushes, and lowering the noisy little creatures to the surface, to keep them away from the living quarters of the children, and adults, that both the milk and meat supply, and the humans who fed upon them, would be safe from predators.

For now, the chickens would remain with the rest, but next order of business was to give each separate pens.

And soon, they would plant the fruit trees, and the gardens...

In the future, they would have eggs, pork, goat meat, milk, fruit and vegetables. Already, they had found edible fruit growing. The men would hunt, set traps...they first had to make weapons.

But, they would survive!

It should all be ready, when the young ones were old enough.

Gem could hear the dinosaurs in the distance, the large cats, and wolves, calling to, or threatening, each other. She was glad that Loni, and the other men had so prepared ahead. They were above ground, and safe.

The Hydra had vanished, unable to get to them, for the sewer ended at the cliff. Off in the distance, when it was light, you could see the many mountain peaks, each the head of a dome, each one smoking, as the damage had spread throughout the system. Until the poisonous air had dissipated, it would be unsafe to scavenge deep within the earth. There would be no more rescues, nothing.

Besides, every once in a while, the ground still shook with tremors.

Also, if ever they were to venture back in, a new bridge back to the ledge needed to be built. They need not hurry with that.

Scar was quite willing to remain with them, and they to forgive him, but even he, felt the guilt of the many deaths he had caused. He resided, either with his barnyard collection, or in a housing dome by himself...he was the only one who seemed unhappy.

About the Author:

If anything, Margaret Afseth is a survivor. She spent most of 2014 battling Cancer, a tumor pressing on the optic nerve. Now she counts herself among the rare few who, in her words, conquered the 'Beastie'. Though now sight restricted, with the aid of her daughter to publish, she continues to write.

From an early age, she was making up stories. While raising her four children alone, she wrote her first novel...in long hand. Unfortunately, she gave the only copy of the manuscript to someone of the opinion, she should not be writing at all. He burned it.

Discouraged, she went underground, not surfacing again until her senior years, when at the age of seventy, 2013, she rewrote and published, as a three part series, the lost novel, calling it The Aopato Chronicles.

Since then, Margaret has gone on to write the Noor Chronicles, published 2014, the last book of which was written while she was undergoing Chemo and Radiation treatment.

In her next set of novels, the Deception series, much of what is wrong in our medical system is mirrored...

Margaret is a widow, with four grown children, five grandchildren, and one great grandchild. Her experience comes not from academic education, but from the great reservoir of knowledge, gained from observing human nature.

Discover other titles by Margaret Afseth at Amazon.com

Aopato book 1(Aopato Chronicles)

Remedy book 2(Aopato Chronicles)

Turn Back book 3(Aopato Chronicles)

Hidden From View(a short story)

Gentle Beast book 1(Noor Chronicles)

Soul Saver book 2(Noor Chronicles)

Healer Nest book 3(Noor Chronicles)

If you enjoyed this book, here is a sample of book two of the Deception Series, coming soon:

FIRE AND ICE

By

Margaret Afseth

PROLOGUE:

Three tiny treasures,

Fragile new life;

Two golden brown;

The last blue as ice.

First one orphaned,
Second forcibly taken;
Third scarcely living,
But none forsaken.

Two speak as one,
Mind words too fast;
First understands not,
Yet has knowledge from the past.

Bring these together,
Whether sister or not,
Seeking a weapon?
Beware! Better not!

Chapter 1

Brad was not going to grieve; he simply was too angry! She should not have died like that! She had cancer...brain cancer! She wasn't supposed to drowned, especially not way out in some ocean.

What was the plane doing in the Bermuda Triangle, anyway? That is nowhere near the coast of Canada where they were supposed to be heading.

But that was where they had just recently found the empty shell of the plane...at the bottom of the ocean, on the opposite side of the world.

And now, he was in a grave yard, with his motherless daughter, burying an empty box in a tiny square hole in the ground...so they could finally, have a place to bring flowers...and mourn.

They would place a slab of concrete over the hole, a marker that read with her name, and call it her grave, but...

No way! I won't believe she's dead, until I see her body! And...I'll go to the bottom of that ocean to find it, if I have to...whether it takes me the rest of my life, or not! I won't come back until I can bring her home with me!

Chapter 2

From an early age she had always been told, she had never actually been born. At seven months formed, a Physician aborted her.

Nitha's first vague memories were of probes and forceps; being cut away from inside her mother...the gushing blood; and gasping at air...

They first grew her in a test box until she was large enough to breathe on her own...and suckle...

But, then...she had been rescued...

She remembered her real daddy's great, giant hands ripping her from that glass and metal chamber, removing the tubes, needles, and wires, then soothing her, holding her, naked and shivering, cuddled against his huge chest.

I can still feel that first touch...if I concentrate...

She'd been told, Papa was brown. Momma Jewel has pink skin, and that is why Nitha's is a golden-brown...a combination of them both.

Papa had been simple, and couldn't talk; her real Momma stutters...because of that, Nitha too, rarely speaks.

The Scientists had been experimenting on her; as a result Nitha developed into a telepath.

In Papa's thoughts, she had always been his belly bump. His was the first mind she had ever entered.

Now, her best friend, Thea, talks for her; they communicate mind to mind. That's how Nitha learned to vocalize out loud.

Proudly, Nitha thinks:

We are as sisters; though each is from a different momma.

Thea laughingly cuts in:

Momma Gem calls us girls, Fire and Ice...

All six of us, the four boys, and us two girls, have two mommas between us, but...just one Papa...

Daddy Da died shortly after her birth, as he tried to carry away the boys...

That dreadful Hydra monster got him!

Silence followed. Finally Nitha added:

There is another coming. She will complete the circle...

"Say what? You see that? In the future? Is it a baby?"

Nitha shook her head.

No!

TO READ MORE GO TO AMAZON.COM